THE YOWLER FOUL-UP

THE ILLMOOR CHRONICLES

BOOK TWO

THE YOWLER FOUL-UP

DAVID LEE STONE

HYPERION BOOKS FOR CHILDREN

NEW YORK

Hyperion Books for Children,
114 Fifth Avenue, New York, New York 10011-5690.
First published in the U.K. by Hodder's Children's Books.
First U.S. Edition, 2006
1 3 5 7 9 10 8 6 4 2
Designed by Christine Kettner
Printed in the United States of America
Reinforced binding
Library of Congress Cataloging-in-Publication Data on file.
ISBN 0-7868-5597-5
Visit www.hyperionbooksforchildren.com

For my grandmother,
Doris Christina Stone
And my late grandfather,
David Stone

SELECTED DRAMATIS PERSONAE

(ye cast of characters)

BARROWBIRD: A distant relative of the forest hornbill

BOWLCOCK, LORD: First ruler of Dullitch (deceased)

COLDWELL, JED: A gravedigger

CURFEW, RAVIS: A viscount; Lord of Dullitch

DAFISFUL, GRAB: A thief

EDWY: A Yowler acolyte

FJIN, FROWD: Landlord of the Rotting Ferret

HALVN: An elf guard

HOPKIRK, FLICKA: Fogrise aide, daughter of
Lord Modeset's secretary

INNKEEPER: Owner of the Steeplejack Inn

LADY LAURIS; THE LARK: A Yowler priestess

LOPSALM: A Yowler curate

MARSHALL, PEGRAND: Manservant to Duke Modeset

MIXER: A gnome

MODESET, VANDRE: A disgraced noble, former
Duke of Dullitch

MOORS: A Yowler acolyte

MULDOON, WRICKSHAW: A sorcerer

OBEGARDE, JARETH: A loftwing investigator

QUICKSTINT, JIMMY: A thief turned gravedigger

SORROW, ALAN: Dullitch quartermaster

SPIRES, MILQUAY: Secretary to Viscount Curfew

VRUNAK, AUGUSTUS: An inventor

An extract from the memoirs of Vandre Modeset,
forty-third Duke of Dullitch:

*The lowest of the low. Destitute. Exiled from Dullitch along
with my personal manservant, Pegrand, I returned to my
birthplace: the forest kingdom of Fogrise. There I was
happily reunited with Hopkirk, elderly retainer of the Keep
and my father's own secretary. Together with these loyal aides
and Hopkirk's indomitable daughter, Flicka, I determined to
restore the kingdom to the grandeur it had once enjoyed....*

*It was a time of brief happiness and, without the chaos
of city duties, Pegrand and I grew to become good friends.*

*Little did I suspect that fate was set to urinate on my
doorstep once more. Just five months later, I lost my beloved
ancestral home in a complicated and particularly ruthless game
of Snap.*

*Now we have been forced to sink to new depths of
poverty, and the others are becoming increasingly despon-
dent. However, I remain optimistic about the future; I'm
certain that something will turn up soon....*

PROLOGUE

MORNING SUNLIGHT flooded Illmoor.

In the south it bathed the Gleaming Mountains and the fifteen spires of Dullitch, city capital of the continent. In the north it infiltrated the sprawling forest of Grinswood, home to a variety of magic sects, including the Dark Trinity.

The Dark Trinity was nothing more than a name, a pronouncement. The Druids who made up its order were not in the least given over to darkness, but had simply been tarred by their proximity to the black heart of the wood. They served and represented Jort, God of Animal Kinship, a hypocritical entity famously disgraced when the King of the Gods paid him a surprise visit and found his sitting room full of deer heads.

The order occupied Jort's Hand, a fortified

manse in the center of the wood, and a place only marginally less attractive than the decrepit moss that clung to its walls. The spiral towers of Jort's Hand rose high above the forest roof, and had stood solid against the wrath of time and the onslaught of the area's changeable weather. Only the skyward towers caught the sunlight, due to the unique way in which the trees huddled together and locked branches. This meant the forest floor was always dark, although occasionally a few flashes of daylight would slip through the net of foliage and illuminate a daffodil. The effect was rather less than ethereal.

The Dark Trinity seldom took an interest in local affairs and few could blame them, considering the area. It was difficult to preach forest lore to a tribe whose only encounters with the animal kingdom came as a result of hunger. Occasionally, when the goblins killed a goat, or the trolls ambushed a wolf pack, the Dark Trinity would be called upon to intervene. These were sad and desperate times, and too many species were dwindling into extinction. Chief among these was the group of giant lizards, known locally as the Batchtiki.

The Batchtiki, although unspeakably rare, were not worth much to anybody; their skins were rough and uncomfortable to wear, and their one talent relied heavily upon their being alive to perform it. Therefore, when a forest interloper (at no small risk to his health) was observed stealing a group of baby lizards from their nest in the northeastern corner of the forest, the Dark Trinity was immediately concerned. However, being of sound mind, and suspecting, quite correctly, that this intruder was merely a pawn for some higher intelligence, they dispatched a barrowbird, one cursed to remain forever in the service of Jort, to spy for them and to trace the theft to its source. . . .

The bird's mission, unbeknownst to the order at that time, would end in the cobbled streets of Dullitch, which seemed like a lifetime away. It would begin . . .

PART ONE

THE
GREAT RETURNING

ONE

 . . . $\mathcal{S}$OMEWHERE IN THE northeastern corner of the forest. A tiny sprite emerged from the gloomy depths of a tree hollow and listened, translucent wings fluttering in the midmorning breeze. A boot crushed it into the ground.

The thief was out of breath. He had run the length of Grinswood in just under three hours, which was a boastful feat for a man on horseback, let alone one with three broken toes, a limp, and advanced constipation. He staggered, muttered a few obscenities, and collapsed in a final wave of exhaustion, dropping his prize beside him. The sack wriggled as it hit the floor, and continued to do so for several minutes. Then it seemed to give up. The rest of the glade was still, with only the thief's heaving chest and slow, determined breaths punctuating the silence.

Time passed. . . .

Presently, a barrowbird flew into the glade, landing on the gnarled lower branches of an ancient oak. It cocked its head to one side and considered the scene.

The thief, whose distinguishing features included one mechanical arm and a moon-shaped scar dissecting his chin, struggled to raise a charred eyebrow. The commotion inside the sack had started up again and even appeared to be building; yet he took no notice.

Still, the bird watched.

A few minutes later, the thief had taken to rolling around on the grass in a number of failed attempts to get to his feet. Finally, he made a desperate lunge at the oak, twisted around, and shouldered himself up. Blood rushed to his head as he fought to maintain his balance.

The barrowbird, completely nonplussed by the sudden display of energy, fixed its beady eyes on the sack.

Grinswood had become eerily silent. Shadows merged, and the trees seemed to move with them.

The thief took one last look around. "Time to move," he muttered, snatching up the sack and urging himself into a run.

When he'd disappeared from view, the barrow-bird twitched and ruffled its feathers. Then it flew up onto a higher branch and cast a glance down the forest path, where a trail of disturbed foliage marked the thief's progress.

I'll take my time, it thought. *This one looks like he's come a long way.*

TWO

For the specific attention of Duke Vandre Modeset,
Fourth Kennel Along,
Fechit's Dog Sanctuary,
Fogrise.

Dearest Cousin,
I was delighted to hear from the redoubtable Pegrand that
you have decided to accept my offer of hospitality. It has
been some months since the terms of your exile entitled you
to return to Dullitch, albeit as a citizen!

    I can assure you that the "rat catastrophe" is a long-
forgotten piece of Dullitch history; people have moved on! I
do so look forward to seeing you and, to this end, have
taken the liberty of booking you four rooms at the
Steeplejack Inn, a grand boardinghouse on Royal Road. I
trust your visit, along with that of your staff, will be both
enjoyable and relaxing.

Regards,
Your cousin, Ravis Curfew, Lord of Dullitch

Duke Modeset had read the letter many times, and was still of the opinion that it had probably been written by one of the palace's many scribes. As far as he was concerned, anyone who described Pegrand as redoubtable probably didn't have a royal bone in his body.

He sighed, folded the letter neatly in two, and looked around for somewhere to file it. His gaze eventually came to rest on something that he assumed was supposed to be a bureau. A curious piece of furniture, it looked as if the carpenter responsible had started out with high hopes but had evidently been sidetracked en route to perfection. Modeset reached down to open the drawer and scowled as the handle broke off. Shoddy. Oh well, at least the place felt like home. He tried and failed to replace the handle three times before letting it fall to the floor, where it clattered noisily on the wooden boards. He propped the parchment on the windowsill instead.

Despite the cracked plaster and crumbling beams, there could be little doubt that the Steeplejack Inn was indeed a five-star resort; the only problem being that a five-star resort in Dullitch was the equivalent of a mutant cesspool anywhere else on the continent. Modeset wasn't sure what the minimum requirements were for earning five stars, but Spittle Bridge had three, and there was water under *that*.

Modeset crossed to the bed, turned, and let himself fall back onto the mattress. The moment he did, there was an explosion of sound much like a dwarf war-hammer hitting a wardrobe door. Pain ricocheted through Modeset's back, and he sat up with a start. His eyes bulged.

A moment later, the duke's faithful manservant erupted through the bedroom door. His face was redder than a beetroot.

"You all right, milord?" he wheezed, leaning against the door frame for support.

The duke, still grasping his back, glared at him.

"Only, did you hear that almighty bang?"

Modeset nodded.

"So did we. What was it, d'you reckon?"

"It was me, Pegrand," Modeset managed, suppressing a groan. "Go and tell the innkeeper that I want another bed. This mattress is thinner than your anorexic aunt."

"I'll have a word in his ear, milord."

"Good man. Where's your room?"

Pegrand pointed skyward. " 'Snot exactly Marble Heights, though," he confided, lowering his voice to a whisper. "There's a big leak in the roof. The innkeeper says it doesn't let much in, but I've been speaking to a few of the guests and they reckon the last bloke who stopped in the attic drowned. I dunno how the others're getting on."

Modeset put his head in his hands and tried to focus on the positives. Firstly, he was on holiday. That, generally speaking, was a good thing. He was accompanied by a full complement of personal staff, which was another. Negatively speaking, the inn was a dump; the city, a nightmare he'd spent the best part of seven years trying to forget; and the staff, a pair of depraved cultural dropouts from a depressing backwater he couldn't wait to forget. Then there was Pegrand. He imagined a series of public humiliations and disastrous misunderstandings festering on the horizon, and he determined to escape before they arrived. After all, fate was avoidable; it was destiny that caused trouble.

THREE

MODESET CHECKED his pocket watch. There was still half an hour to go before dinner. Having already paced back and forth in his room for what seemed like a millennium, he decided to take a nap. He carefully lowered himself onto the bed, worked his body into a halfway comfortable position, and tried to drift off.

CRASH!

His eyes flicked open, and he sat bolt upright.

The inner shutters were devastated; one had been wrenched off its hinges and the other had slammed into the far wall with such velocity that it had spawned a network of cracks in the plaster.

For a moment the duke observed the rules of stunned silence and remained absolutely still. Then he leaped off the bed and hurried over to the window.

The street below was dark and shadowy, and the bleak light offered by the lamp wicks betrayed no obvious signs of an explosion.

And so it begins, he thought bitterly. Word of my arrival has got around and suddenly everyone's out wandering the streets with a brick in each hand. Ha! So much for moving on!

He peered cautiously out of the window, expecting at any second to be bombarded by the rest of someone's garden wall.

Nothing: the street was empty. Silence reigned. From what he could make out, the rest of Royal Road's crooked buildings were largely undisturbed. There was a fire blazing somewhere to the north, but nothing to account for the sudden, meteoric destruction of the shutters.

Modeset sighed and pulled the outer shutter closed. He was about to return to bed when he saw the rock on the floor beside the bureau. It was wrapped in parchment which, in turn, was fastened with string. For a moment he just stared at the rock, as if waiting for it to sprout legs and run under the door.

Then he sighed despondently, bent down, and tried to pick it up, groaning when it turned out to be a stone heavier than the average cannonball.

Puffing and panting with effort, he hefted the rock onto the bed, untied the string, and folded out the parchment. There was a note on the back.

Modeset squinted at the writing, which was crude and betrayed a certain loathing for punctuation. It certainly wasn't what he expected:

ToNight WAS a tASTer There iS MoRE to coME StaY away frOm wareHouse six if You don't yOu Will wAke up FEELing Not vEry well with a cRossbow bolT iN Your bAck yOu have beEN warned there are many ToRture instruMEnts whICH wE Are NOT aFraid to uSe in aN EmerGeNcY aNd we knoW yOuR arE A lOFtWing bECAuSe YOu ONly folloW at niGHT aNd We hAve lots oF SiLvEr WhicH KiLLS YOu lOT So BE wArNEd

No More OuT of YOU aFTer thAT thEn MisTeR X (ANd thatS NOT My ReAL naME SO DoN'T ThiNK YOU'VE GoT Me theRE.)

Modeset looked from the rock to the note and back again, his attention finally diverting to the window. The remaining inward shutter broke off from its hinge and crashed onto the floorboards. He was about to hide the note under the bed when there was a heavy-handed knock on the bedroom door.

"Milord?"

Modeset started, thrust the parchment under his pillow, and pulled the bedcovers over the cannon-ball rock.

"Yes?" he shouted testily. "What is it, Pegrand?"

"Dinner's in five minutes, milord. Thought you might like a quick reminder.

"Mmm? Oh, yes. Thank you."

"No problem. Just yell if you need anything else."

"Good show. I'll be along presently."

"Okay, milord. No worries, then. Everything all right in there, is it? Only, I thought I heard a noise."

"Yes, that was me, Pegrand. I . . . tried to close the wardrobe."

"You've got a wardrobe in there now, milord? That's a first-class accommodation."

Modeset looked around frantically. "No!" he yelled. "It . . . fell out of the window, I'm afraid. Look, I'll be out in a few moments."

"Right you are, milord."

When the manservant's footsteps had dissipated, Modeset snaked a hand under the pillow and retrieved the parchment. After a second reading, he rolled it up and stowed it away inside his tunic. He had a funny feeling that it was going to be one of those nights.

FOUR

ELSEWHERE.

From the state of the room, you could tell it was part of a hovel in one of the seedier parts of the city. The furniture was threadbare, the walls were collapsing, and a dynasty of cockroaches fought terrible wars beneath the floorboards. The occupant of the room, a gnome with brass teeth and a network of terrible scars, was studying something of great importance.

The book stood open on the table. It was a heavy tome, more than five times the size of a regular book, and its pages were inked with bold script and elaborate illustrations. The turning of each leaf was accompanied by a dull crackle, and the gnome spent several moments smoothing the pages down so that the book would close properly. It had to close properly. Otherwise it wouldn't fit in the gap in the wall, and some filthy thief would sneak in and steal it. Such was the norm in Dullitch.

Eventually, when the Ultimate Goal was achieved, he'd move somewhere smaller. Still, that was a long way off, and many parts of the mistress's plan still needed to be realized. Nobody had heard from the lizard thief, yet, and he'd been gone for weeks! Oh well . . . that was definitely not his problem.

The gnome closed the book and stowed it away in the wall, pulling the old, half-rotted dresser in front to conceal it. Then he returned to his little stool and gazed down at an area of the table containing an inkwell, a feathered quill, and a box. This, he reflected, shouldn't be too difficult.

He was certain that Obegarde, the loftwing who'd been following him for two, maybe three days was either from or employed by the palace. Unfortunately, his research hadn't turned up much more than a name, but then, an official palace employee wouldn't be shacked up at a coaching inn.

Hmm . . . a freelancer, then; some sort of investigator. He grimaced at the thought. This was disastrous! How could they possibly have found out?

Mistress Lark had worked at the palace, but it wouldn't have been her, surely? She was much too smart, far too careful. Well, whatever, someone had let slip. Ha! And they'd had the nerve to call *him* stupid. All things considered, it was a miracle the group had managed to keep their little secret at all.

Still, the threat *should* suffice. He certainly hoped it would, because the loftwing was no minor irritant. If the creature found out enough to make a report, he had the potential to ruin everything. It just wasn't fair; he'd been so *careful*!

What to do, what to do . . . ?

First things first: the old inventor. Mistress Lark had been very definite about that; he knew too much and was the most immediate threat to the group. Besides, he was long past being useful; the machine was built and it wasn't likely to go wrong. Even so, assassination *was* a little harsh. Perhaps he should give the old boy a scare, instead. Then he might leave town of his own accord. . . .

Muttering under his breath, the gnome took up the quill and, dipping it into the inkwell, began to write. He folded the parchment into segments, tore neatly along all the edges, and placed a number of blank pieces inside the pockets of a dark cloak he'd stolen, keeping hold of the original piece he'd written on. Then he took the quill *and* its grimy inkwell.

There, he thought. That's just about everything.

Fastening his cloak about him, the gnome hurried from the hovel. It was going to be a busy night. . . .

FIVE

WHEN MODESET reached the first-floor landing, most of his staff was already out in force.

Pegrand was dressed in the standard leather britches and scruffy doublet he always wore, hair spilling out from behind his ears while managing to avoid the top of his head completely. Flicka, Hopkirk's daughter, and the only member of Modeset's staff still enjoying her twenties, had settled for a pure white robe that made her look more like a sacrifice for Druids than a royal aide. Her long dark hair, pale skin, and delicate elfin features were somewhat marred by the quizzical expression that had camped out on her face since the day she was born.

The two of them constituted quite a picture. Modeset didn't think much of the presentation, but then, judging by their collective stare, they were just as disgusted by his choice of formal dress. He couldn't for the life of him understand why; the armored suit might be old, but at least it wasn't paid for.

"Now, this evening represents my first experience of Dullitch hospitality for some time," he said. "I want everyone to make a conscious effort, and that includes you, Pegrand."

"Yes, milord. Got some impressive jokes lined up for the after-dinner discussions."

"None of your sledgehammer wit, please."

"No, milord. Right you are, then. I'll keep a zip on the monkey gag until the crockery's collected. Do we know how many other guests are coming?"

"Not many, I fear. It's just us, the landlord, and supposedly one other gentleman. We're getting special treatment by order of the throne. As I understood it, most of the guests are confined to their rooms until after the meal."

"Should be okay, then, as long as they don't try to dig themselves out. Who's the jailer?"

"I don't find that even remotely amusing, Pegrand."

"Sorry, milord."

"And how about you, Flicka?" said Modeset. "All ready for your first dinner in Dullitch?"

Flicka swept back a lock of her long, ebony hair and fixed Modeset with her sparkly blue eyes. "Do I have any choice?" she said.

"Good, good." Modeset beamed. "We'll descend the stairs in single file. Ladies first," he said. "That's you, Flicka, just in case there's any doubt. I noticed Pegrand took a step forward then and, while he undoubtedly has the tongue of a washerwoman, he is by no means a lady."

Flicka rolled her eyes and took to the stairs.

"Mind your head on that candelabra as you go," the duke called out. "Very tasteful, isn't it?"

"Milord?"

"Yes, okay, Pegrand. Down you go, then. Be sure to announce me as soon as you get to the dining hall . . . and no silly voices this time, I implore you."

SIX

AUGUSTUS VRUNAK had just climbed into bed when the doorbell clanged. Nobody else in Dullitch would have had such bad luck, he thought bitterly. And he was right: nobody else in Dullitch had a doorbell. Such was the price of being an inventor in a city that never sleeps. He'd rigged up the device on a rope-pulley system that ran from the entrance door of his cottage to a bracket above his bedroom door.

He grimaced, swore under his breath, and waited for the small brass tinkle to subside.

Clank, clink, clink, clink;
Clank, clink, clink;
Clank, clink;
CLANG, clank, clink, clink, clink.

Augustus scowled. Whoever it was, they obviously had no intention of waiting until the morning to see him. He climbed out of bed, padded over to the window in his slippers, and peered out at the front lawn. Unusual: his mystery visitor had closed the gate after himself. Perhaps it was his sister. She'd spent most of the evening having dinner with him, and he supposed she might have forgotten something.

CLANG, clank, clink, clink.

"Okay, for goodness' sake!" Augustus bellowed. "I'm coming."

He pulled a dressing gown over his nightshirt and went downstairs, muttering under his breath. On the way down, he glanced into his stairway mirror and reflected, rather bitterly, that he was beginning to look like a chubby old walrus. Oh well, age tended to do that to you. . . .

Odd: the front door was stuck.

He put all his weight behind his heels and leaned back, but the door just wouldn't budge. He spat on his hands and tried again, then put one foot against the frame and heaved with all his might. Nothing happened. Either damp had expanded the wood in a ludicrously short space of time or—he hesitated to think of the alternative—somebody else was pulling from the other side.

The brass bell clanged again, and Augustus suddenly felt extremely cold and alone.

"Is there anybody there?" he called.

He looked down. A small square of paper had been pushed underneath the door. There was writing on it. He reached down carefully and picked it up, one eye on the door in case an axe head came through it.

The paper was perfectly cut, an exact rectangle. He read:

STAND AWAY FROM THE DOOR AUGUSTUS WE
HAVE HOLD OF IT

His mind raced. The Yowlers? It had to be; they were the only ones with a reason.

Sweat began to form on the inventor's brow, and he found himself shivering.

"What do you want from me?" he called.

A second sheet was slipped onto the mat. Augustus read:

DO NOT ATTEMPT TO MAKE A BREAK FOR THE
BACK DOOR EITHER WE ARE THERE ALSO AND
WILL KILL YOU ON SIGHT

"But why? I haven't done anything wrong!"

He bent down to retrieve the answer. Were they

attempting to get to him through his arthritis?

YOU HAVE BEEN TALKING HAVEN'T YOU

TALKING TO AN ENEMY OF THE GROUP

He stood back, thrust his hands into his robe pockets and swallowed. "No," he said. "I never!"

BE VERY CAREFUL HOW YOU ANSWER AUGUSTUS

"There's no need for that kind of talk. I'm already afraid."

YOU SHOULD BE LISTENING WITH INTENT

TOMORROW MORNING YOU WILL PACK YOUR

THINGS AND LEAVE DULLITCH DESTROY ANY

REMAINING EVIDENCE OF YOUR UNION WITH US

BEFORE YOU DEPART PLACE YOUR FRONT-DOOR

KEY UNDER THE FLOWERPOT

Augustus cocked his head to one side. "I don't have a flowerpot."

There was a brief pause before the note appeared.

A FLOWERPOT WILL BE PROVIDED

"Do I get a plant with it?"

YOU ARE SKATING ON VERY THIN ICE AUGUSTUS

"Sorry; didn't mean any disrespect. Go on."

UNDERSTAND THAT AFTER TONIGHT YOU MUST

NEVER SPEAK OF THIS EVENT UNTIL THE DAY

YOU DIE

Augustus gave this a moment's thought. "When will that be?" he asked.

WHENEVER YOU DECIDE TO SPEAK OF THIS EVENT

"Ah," said the inventor. "Now I'm getting you." He pulled his robe tightly around himself and leaned against the door of his broom closet.

HAVE WE ESTABLISHED A MUTUAL TRUST DO YOU THINK

"Yes. I'll do as you say."

YOU ARE A SENSIBLE MAN AUGUSTUS VRUNAK

Time passed. At length, the inventor put one ear to the door. "You still there?" he called.

Silence.

He turned the handle and cautiously peered out into the night. The garden was empty. It showed no sign of having been disturbed, apart from the rusty gate that swung loose in the wind.

SEVEN

THE GRAND DINNER to welcome the return of Duke Modeset began badly and looked like it would be going downhill from there. The innkeeper, a stout man of indefinite age, was unfathomably moody. He mumbled recognizable obscenities under his breath and slammed the dishes down with such fervor that they almost bounced. Moreover, he didn't bother to introduce the other guest, who arrived late and chose a seat so far from the party, they could only communicate with him by sign language.

Eventually, after a number of ignored questions and a few embarrassed silences, they managed to discover the root of the innkeeper's anxiety. It turned out that, despite a promised advance from Viscount Curfew, he had yet to be paid for the party's stay. The duke spent some time assuring him that the bills would be settled, but the innkeeper seemed utterly disgusted with the group, sneering every time one of them reached for a plate. Modeset fancied that the only thing keeping the innkeeper from turning the group onto the streets was a fear of reprisal from the crown. Consequently, a very uncomfortable meal ensued.

"Um, I say, isn't this nice?" Modeset lied. "It's been so long since I've sampled the delicacies of capital cuisine! As I was saying to Flicka, here, I really should get out and see the city again; I've almost forgotten what it looks like! She's young, of course, probably wouldn't be interested in culture. I doubt if the palace would make the Flicka list of places to see! Ha-ha-ha!"

"The palace!" muttered the innkeeper. "Now, there's an idea. Why don't you all go and bloody stay *there*?"

"I'm interested in culture if it involves magic," said Flicka, bringing a dark veil of silence over the table. "I've always been interested in that. In fact, Father got me got this spellbook in Spittle. It's only theory, of course, but I've learned a lot."

"Are you interested in anything *else*, Flicka?"

Modeset prompted, trying to drag the subject away from illegalities. "After all, Dullitch is a very big pla—"

"As a matter of fact I am, Lord M. What about the Yowlers? It amazes me how a city can function with a criminally insane cult thriving beneath it."

"Yes, well, enough of—"

"I mean," she went on, "apart from the forgers at Counterfeit House, I understand there's something called the Rooftop Runners, is that right? Thieves and the like, aren't they?"

"I'd really rather we didn't talk about it," Modeset snapped. "Besides, the Yowlers were born out of an obscure religion, and religion has always been a dicey subject here in Dullitch. I recall a time, not so long ago, when virgins not much older than yourself were chained to rocks and sacrificed for the greater glory of some bizarre god."

"I reckon you might be thinkin' o' Druidics, there, milord," said Pegrand.

"No," Flicka interrupted. "That's definitely how the Yowlers started—"

"I'm telling you, it was—"

An argument ensued.

Modeset, practically unconscious with boredom,

tried to relieve the monotony by watching the stranger at the far end of the table devouring a salad. The man appeared to be having terrible trouble with his meal, spitting out every mouthful of lettuce mere seconds after forking it in. There's a fellow with a few problems, if I'm not mistaken, he thought. When the stranger looked up suddenly, Modeset returned his attention to the argument, and was about to interrupt Pegrand's incessant banter, when a resounding boom from the far end of the table cut through the meal like a rogue scimitar.

"IS THERE GARLIC ON THIS?" it said.

The innkeeper leaned around Pegrand to peer over at the stranger.

"Eh? What's that you're saying? Come over here, will you?"

The stranger lifted his plate and moved several places down the table, nodded and muttered "Evening" at everyone as he took a new seat. He was thickset but looked incredibly sharp; he was also covered in cuts and bruises.

"I said," he began, eyeing the innkeeper dubiously, "did you put garlic on this salad?"

The innkeeper nodded. "A bit, for the flavor. Sorry, I forgot."

"Oh, right. Can I have some of this chicken instead, or is there garlic on everything?"

"Chicken's fine; fresh from the oven."

The stranger reached over to cut off a slice, and almost melted in the heat of Pegrand's stare.

I reckon you must be a vampire, Pegrand's stare seemed to say.

The stranger smiled pleasantly at the manservant, cursing his own ability to read thoughts at close range. He wondered if, just once, it might work both ways. *Why don't you bugger off and die, you filthy, stinking little piece of excrement?*

Pegrand's continued grin indicated that his own ability to read thoughts was still a long way off.

"Yes, I am," the stranger said, instead. "Part vampire, on my mother's side, which unfortunately means I've just the one fang, I only drink blood when there's no wine going, and I can't sleep a wink past midnight. The name's Obegarde. Delighted, I'm sure."

Apart from the innkeeper, who continued to scowl at the empty spaces on the meat tray, every face at the table took on a kind of blank, isolated stare.

Fantastic, thought Modeset. Not only am I living on promised means at a five-star hotel with holes in the roof, and not only am I the mistaken target for some rock-throwing lunatic with a grudge, *now* I'm having dinner with a vampire.

"If it bothers you, I'll go back and sit over there," said Obegarde, pointing toward the far end of the table.

"N-no, nonsense, er, wouldn't hear of it," said the duke. "This here is Pegrand, my manservant, and Flicka Hopkirk, my secretary's somewhat *argumentative* daughter. I'm—"

"Modeset," Obegarde interrupted. "Yes, I remember your reign very well. Lot of rats about, I recall."

"Yes, well, have some wine and a few of those grapes. Make yourself welcome."

"Thank you," said Obegarde, trying as hard as everyone else to ignore the innkeeper's incessant mumbling.

"I wasn't sure I'd be welcome," Obegarde continued. "Some people can be a little hostile."

"Doesn't bother me," Pegrand cut in. "Part undead on your mother's side, you say? Isn't there a name for that? Lowdown or somethin' similar?"

Here we go, thought Modeset. Now he's going to get us all killed.

"I assume the name you're thinking of is 'loftwing,' " Obegarde replied, taking up the wine bottle and emptying it into a clean glass. "But it's a spiteful word and I don't find it very flattering. Besides, we don't have much in common with the dark breed; all of the longevity and none of the class, so to speak."

Modeset had practically turned to stone. His thoughts raced to the rolled parchment still concealed in his tunic. So that's who the note was meant for, he thought. Whoever threw the rock must have intended it for the vampire and thrown it through the wrong window. Interesting.

Pegrand sniffed and nodded. "Must be a borin' old stretch for you lot," he said. "Moochin' through a hundred lifetimes in the darkness while the rest of us peg out. What do you do with yourself?"

Obegarde, who'd been looking sideways at Modeset with a curious expression on his face, gave the manservant a sudden, impassive smile.

"I'm an investigator," he said. "I specialize in looking for people who don't want to be found."

A number of eyebrows were raised.

"How d'you know?" said Pegrand.

"Mmm?"

"Well, these people you're looking for. How d'you know they don't want to be found?"

The vampire considered this. "Well," he said eventually. "It's obvious, isn't it? I can't find them easily."

"Yeah, but that could just be you."

"Ha-ha! Yes, I suppose it could. No, in fact, it's just a polite way of saying that my job involves a lot of confrontation."

"Ah, I see," said Pegrand. "That explains why you look like you just spent an hour in a dustbin full o' kittens."

Kill him, thought Modeset. Please, do us all a favor. Leap across the table and rip his throat out.

Obegarde smiled, but said nothing.

"I'm sure Mr. Obegarde would rather not discuss his business at the dinner table," Modeset interrupted, glaring with intensity when he saw the look on Pegrand's face. "Client confidentiality, and all that."

There was a general murmur of agreement, and a few smaller pockets of conversation rippled between the staff and the innkeeper.

Eventually, the innkeeper struggled to his feet and shuffled off toward the kitchens. Modeset made a gesture for Pegrand to follow suit, but the manservant had nodded off. Flicka collected the crockery instead. The atmosphere, which had been hovering over the table like a big black cloud, finally lifted.

"*Sooooo*," said Obegarde, prolonging the word until everyone still conscious was out of earshot. "Where is it, then? This message that was so obviously meant for me?"

Modeset frowned. "I've absolutely no idea what you're talking about."

"Oh don't bother with all that rubbish," snapped Obegarde. "I read your mind."

There was a moment of silence.

"Very well," said the duke, keeping one eye on the little wooden door to the kitchens. He put a hand inside his tunic and produced the roll of parchment.

Obegarde snatched it from him. "Good," he said. "Now, I'd appreciate it if you forgot the contents."

He finished chewing on his chicken leg and tossed it onto a plate heaped high with leftovers.

Modeset shrugged. "I confess I'm quite intrigued," he said. "It doesn't sound as if the chap's too interested in talking."

Obegarde got to his feet. Modeset was surprised

at the size of the man. Somehow, one expects vampires to be thin and gaunt. Obegarde looked like an athletic ogre.

"There's more to it than that," he said. "And, with respect, none of it's any of your business, your *lordship*."

Modeset was slow to nod.

"Nice to have met you," said Obegarde. He stood, returned to his original seat, and pulled on his overcoat. "Thank Grumpy for the meal, will you?"

He turned and swept from the room, coattails billowing out behind him.

Modeset watched the vampire go, and swallowed. Betrayed by my own mind, he thought. Whatever next?

"Mmmff, Morris! Where's the cauldron?" said Pegrand still immersed in his dream. He woke with a ghoulish yawn and stared about with sudden panic. "What? Where'd I go?"

"You drifted off, Pegrand," said Modeset, finishing his wine. "Happens to the best of us."

The manservant managed a lopsided grin.

"Ah, sorry about that, milord," he said. "Did I miss much?"

"Nothing," the duke replied, lowering his wineglass onto the tabletop. "Nothing at all."

EIGHT

MIST WAS DESCENDING on the streets of Dullitch, swirling around the ancient lampposts and lending a mysterious haze to the normality of midnight. In the cemetery, a light flickered between the gravestones, becoming more and more erratic as the wind began to pick up. Someone was digging.

Jimmy Quickstint scooped up a generous pile of earth with his rusty shovel, struggling to keep the tool level while countless grains poured over the sides in a brown avalanche. Then, employing a deft flick of the wrist, he spun the shovel one hundred and eighty degrees, depositing the dirt on a growing pile beside the plot. An old weather-beaten lamp perched jauntily over the grave.

Several scoops later, gasping with a mixture of relief and exhaustion, Jimmy Quickstint drove the shovel hard into the dirt, embedding it in the soil so deeply that it remained upright. He mopped his sweating brow with the sleeve of his overalls and looked up at his superior.

The old man was sitting on the grassy bank nearby, filling a dingy brown pipe with small shags of rough tobacco. He went through this same routine every night, regular as clockwork. It was one of the man's many habits that drove his apprentice insane; that, and the fact that he never actually seemed to do any work.

"Finished," Jimmy called over the lip of the open grave.

"Aye," came the short reply.

"Should I climb out now?"

"Aye."

"Should I drown in a pool of my own blood?"

"Aye."

Jimmy rolled his eyes and, after a number of unsuccessful attempts, managed to struggle out of the hole and roll onto level ground.

The old man finished binding the seal of his tobacco pouch with string, and stowed it safely away in the confines of his grubby overcoat. Finally, he seemed to notice his apprentice crouching on the ground before him, gasping for breath by the lungful.

"'Ave you reached ol' Clifford?" the old man asked, scratching the fast-receding hair beneath his flat cap. "If you have, you've gone too far."

Jimmy looked about in bewilderment. "Come again?" he managed.

"I said, ''Ave you reached old Clifford?'"

"Who's Clifford?"

"Him what's buried down that there hole."

"No, sir. *This* is the grave for Mr. Flunk, due in tomorrow. Remember?"

"Aye, and that's as may be, lad, but that there plot is already occupied. You prob'ly 'aven't gone down far enough."

Jimmy looked back into the open grave from which he'd just emerged and shook his head in amazement. "You mean there's someone already down there?" he gasped.

"Aye," the old man confirmed. "'As been these last fifty year or so."

"But, but what about Mr. Flunk? The priests told his family he could go in here!"

"Aye, I know. That's why we gotta get Clifford out, see?"

Jimmy swallowed, struggling against the odds to force back the horror of the situation. "How long has this been going on?" he said.

The old man cocked his head to one side. "Oh, we ran outta room down here a long while back."

"How long? My uncle was buried in this cemetery!"

The old man waved him down in an attempt to restore calm. "Now, don't you fret none, young'un, your uncle's prob'ly still a restin' right where you left him." He sucked in his scraggly lower lip. "An' when was that?"

"About five years ago," said Jimmy, tapping his foot impatiently.

"Ooh, now le' me see, right around the time of— yes, I 'spect he's a few bodies down by now, but he'll be there, right enough."

"A few bodies down? A *few bodies down*? You mean you're burying people one on top of another after what my aunt paid? It's a disgrace." Jimmy screamed, marching off toward the cemetery gates. "That's it! I'm out of here. You can find yourself another slave!"

NINE

Morning arrived, another murky one.

Apart from the Diamond Clock Tower on Crest Hill, Dullitch Palace was easily the largest and most impressively placed structure in the city. The building itself was falling to pieces; though, on a superficial glance from the gates, it retained much of its original grace and beauty (something that, sadly, couldn't be said of the guards).

"What do you mean 'He doesn't want to see me'?" Modeset exclaimed. "I'm his cousin, for goodness' sake. I'm here at his request! I'm royalty!"

"The viscount is busy with matters of state," said the sentry, an aging, thickset elf with crooked teeth and more scars than the tooth fairy (the citizens of Dullitch didn't like to let go of *anything*).

"He's not seeing anyone until the trade war with Legrash is sorted out."

"There is no trade war between Legrash and Dullitch!" the duke snapped. "It's just an excuse to fob off the citizens, and I know that because I invented it! I demand entrance now!"

The duke made a move to step past the guard, and found his way barred by a heavy iron pike.

"What's this?" Modeset demanded. "A peasant uprising?"

"I ain't no peasant," said the guard. "And the only uprising round here's likely to involve you on the end of this."

He indicated the pike head and widened his grin. "Some of us haven't forgot the last time you occupied the palace," he added.

Modeset took a step back, shouldering Pegrand aside in the process.

"Don't let 'em talk to you like that, Lord M!" yelled Flicka, nudging the duke forward with a bemused smile on her face. She'd followed the dynamic duo around the city for the best part of a morning and was now thoroughly sick and tired of the duke's attitude. As far as she could see, it was no use looking down on people who weren't looking up.

Modeset, however, was thinking along the same lines. So far, he'd received the type of hospitality usually reserved for barbarian invaders. What happened to people forgiving and forgetting? At the very least he'd expected a fanfare at Modeset's Fort, a guardhouse originally opened in his honor.

The palace was the last straw. Modeset was beginning to lose patience.

"Pegrand," he said. "You're supposed to be trained in self-defense, aren't you? Teach this insolent fool a lesson he'll never forget!"

The manservant, who'd been retrieving part of the guardhouse biscuit from his teeth with a grimy fingernail, looked suddenly taken aback. "I can't use self-defense unless I'm bein' attacked, milord," he said sheepishly.

Modeset looked astounded. "Don't be ridiculous, man!" he said. "You have to bring preemptive measures into play, don't you see? Provoke the situation! The only way you're ever going to need something like self-defense is if the aggressor comes straight at you, and the only way to ensure that is by hitting him first: like this!"

The duke sprang forward and glanced a blow off the guard's chin. Although lightweight, the punch caught the elf completely by surprise and he flew back, knocking into the portcullis control mechanism. Guards ran in every direction, displaying the sudden panic of men who'd been prepared for mass invasion for so long, they'd actually forgotten what to do in the light of any minor trouble.

The portcullis slammed down.

The guards stopped running, and looked around.

Two blurred shapes were fast receding over the newly erected Gatehouse Bridge. The guards looked at one another, and then they were off, kicking up dust behind them.

Flicka watched the chase until all had disappeared into Palace Street, then she began to follow at a leisurely pace.

TEN

MODESET HAD never run so fast in his life.

Heart pounding, arms pumping, and limbs screaming in submission, he raced along Palace Street as if the entire Dullitch Army were after him. He couldn't think, he couldn't hear and, thanks to the wind, he could only see faint blurs through the watery haze of his tears. More important, though, he was seriously beginning to enjoy himself.

The pair had been together up until the junction of Royal Road. That's where he'd lost Pegrand. A backward glance had seen the manservant shin up an oak tree in the front garden of a rather elegant cottage.

Boots pounded the cobbles.

Modeset peered over his shoulder and saw that

the elf guard he'd punched was leading the pursuit. The enraged, slightly dazed expression on its face suggested that the elf's job description hadn't included taking physical abuse from down-on-their-luck members of the nobility.

The market was in full swing. Modeset made for a tightly packed group of spice stalls on the east side of the square.

On his way past the first stall he grabbed a bowl of blue dust and threw it wide. The bowl spun in the air, spewing a curtain of dust over the front line of guards and two Orcish spice merchants who just happened to be in the way. They waved their fists and shouted gruff obscenities at Modeset but, mercifully, in a dialect he didn't recognize.

Energy waning, the duke ran on, never daring to look behind. He knew that the elf was still in pursuit because of the rhythmic clanking noise its armor made as it ran. Modeset thought that it sounded like an ancient war wagon about to give up the ghost. As if in answer to the thought, the clanking ceased. And the duke made a cardinal mistake: he slowed and turned around.

The elf guard, having suddenly propelled itself into the air in a desperate, last-ditch attempt to catch up, brought Modeset down in a single striking movement.

They rolled over and over on the ground. Despite Modeset's frantic struggles, the guard clearly had the situation well under control. It leaped to its feet and dragged the duke up after it.

"You wanted to see the viscount, right?" it said. "Well, *now* you've got your wish. You can see Lord Curfew immediately. In chains."

The punch wasn't hard, but it caught Modeset completely unawares and knocked him to the ground.

The guard muttered something under his breath and, hefting the duke onto one shoulder, headed back to the palace. On the way, he was stopped by a rather attractive young lady who asked him directions to the market square. He was in the process of describing an ideal route, when she suddenly brought her knee up between his legs and caught him a chop across the back of the neck as he dropped the duke. He didn't remember much after that.

Modeset woke up running. Still groggy from the elf's punch, he felt Flicka running beside him, her arm wedged under his shoulder as support. He was about to congratulate her on the rescue when she suddenly propelled him through a shop doorway so fast, he hit the counter headfirst and almost knocked himself out again. She quickly hurried in after him and slammed the door, ducking down as a group of guards bolted past the window.

Modeset dug his fingernails into the counter and dragged himself to his feet. They were in a toy shop, and the watchword was *clutter*. Every shelf was packed with rocking horses, dollies, teddy bears, and wooden soldiers.

The shopkeeper was so small that Modeset at first mistook him for one of the toys. Modeset had been walking along the counter when an arm shot out to greet him.

"Ah! Welcome to my shop. Would you like a teddy bear?"

Modeset declined the handshake. "Not particularly."

"How about a dolly for your daughter?"

"She's not my daughter and, no, thank you."

"Wooden horse for the young lady?"

"We don't want anything," Modeset snapped, still watching out for the militia.

"Then what did you come in here for?"

"We came in to get away from the guards," said Flicka, stepping up to the counter.

"You're criminals, then!" said the shopkeeper excitedly. "I have just the thing!"

He disappeared behind a small curtain at the back of the shop, returning with his arms full.

"This is a magical dolly from Phlegm. Highly illegal and terribly dangerous in the wrong hands, it excretes acid, is highly inflammable, and also explodes in water."

"That is the most despicable thing I've ever heard of," Modeset snapped, snatching the doll from the shopkeeper's outstretched arms and slamming it down on the counter. "You sell life-threatening toys in this shop? During my reign, I'd have had you hanged for that."

"Your reign? Oh goodness, yes. I thought I recognized you. We do carry stuffed rats, your lordship."

"How amusing."

"What does the teddy do?" asked Flicka, pointing to the small brown bear under the little man's other arm.

"Ahh, now this is Sven, a very magical toy indeed, and not at all dangerous. In fact, if sorcery weren't banned in Dullitch, he'd be perfectly legal. Sven, you see, has an answer for everything."

"Hmm, I remember Sven," Modeset started. "Those were all the rage in Fogrise a few years back. They give you the same stupid answer each time. I think it's usually 'I'm a happy bear,' or something similar."

"Not this one," whispered the shopkeeper. "Try it for yourselves if you don't believe me!"

Flicka looked the bear up and down. "How does it work?"

"Simple! Ask it a question and then draw out the string. It will talk until the cord runs out."

Flicka took the bear, ignoring Modeset's protests, and put her finger through the loop. Then she said, "How much is that doggy in the window?" and let go.

The bear's voice was clear but strangely disquieting. It sounded like a death rattle, and spoke in one long, narrowing breath.

"It's-a-toy-shop-and-there-is-no-doggy-in-the-window-but-if-there-were-and-I'm-not-for-a-second-suggesting-that-there-is-then-it-would-probably-be-one-with-a-waggly-tail."

"That's incredible!" said Flicka, hugging the

bear and turning to the shopkeeper with a pleading grin. "How much is it?"

"Fifty crowns. . . ."

Modeset snatched the bear from Flicka's arms and drew out the cord. "Why are you so damned expensive?" he inquired.

"You-pay-for-quality-in-this-life-so-don't-waste-my-time-pal-there-are-kids-out-there-who-need-answers."

Modeset boggled at the toy and, incredulous, turned to the shopkeeper. "Do you know what I think?" he said. "I think these toys were perfectly ordinary to begin with and then _you_ came along and made despicable alterations to them."

The shopkeeper shook his head emphatically and reached for the bear, but Modeset lifted it beyond his grasp.

"I'll take these two," he said. "And I warn you, there'd better not be any more of them."

He gave the bear and the dolly to Flicka, and had just finished paying for them when the door of the shop flew open and a number of heavily armed militiamen poured in.

ELEVEN

Viscount Curfew didn't smile very often. This fact would have come as no great surprise to the palace clerks: having seen the contessa they were amazed he managed it at all. Lady Curfew had an angular face that came complete with jutting jaw and a forehead which kept her feet dry. She also had watery eyes and thick lips, and something about her stance always gave people the impression of bad indigestion.

Thankfully, there were other amusements in the palace, and the chambermaids were always good for a giggle. In one morning, Curfew had worked his way through kiss-chase, hide-'n'-seek, and a new method of hopscotch that involved leaping over dangerously large statues. He put his appetite for fun down to stress. It was an excuse with which everyone sympathized. Just living in Dullitch did terrible things to people; only the gods knew what a nightmare it must be to run the place.

No, Curfew was a man determined to have fun; a pursuit enjoyed by none of his innumerable predecessors: wretches to a man, the last four in particular warranted scorn. First there had been Lord Morban, the hooded duke, a man so tortured by his own disfigurement that the only time the citizens ever saw his face was at his funeral. Bizarrely, there hadn't been a scratch on him. Lunatic.

Next had come Baron Smother, a stout schizophrenic who despaired when he was given the throne and proceeded to attempt suicide in every one of the palace's forty-seven rooms, finally succeeding with a candlestick in the study. Lunatic.

Then along trundled Edwyn Vitkins, a retired soldier who declared war on Spittle and left to occupy the place before he'd even been sworn in! Thankfully for all concerned, he was dead in a fortnight. Lunatic.

Last but not least, there was Modeset and the oft-fabled rat catastrophe. Ha! Three lunatics and a sadistic incompetent . . . some birthright. And the painting!

Curfew peered up at the poorly finished portrait of Duke Vitkins. The Illmoor nobility approved of interbreeding, partly because of social grace and partly because no one from the streets would have anything to do with them. This culminated in a royal family whose members all looked identical to one another and, consequently, only one portrait hung in the Dullitch throne room. It had seventy-three names underneath it.

Tiring of his surroundings, Curfew had turned to the papers. The news was grim: a statue he'd had erected of himself outside the Candleford Boys' School had not been well received. Condemned by both the press and the public, some parents were claiming that their sons now walked the entire cir-cumference of the city simply to avoid passing it on their way to school.

Curfew was nodding off to sleep at his desk when Spires, administrator to the ducal throne, erupted into the chamber.

"I need to speak with you, Excellency," he said. The ticks, nervous twitches, and various other facial distortions that plagued the man night and day were going into overdrive.

Awakened from his nap, Curfew bolted his

head upright and bellowed, "Don't you ever knock?"

"I'm sorry, Excellency," said Spires quickly. "But this is important. Your cousin Lord Modeset is here and he's requesting an audience."

Curfew rolled his eyes. "Why did we have to invite him back, exactly?"

"It's expected, Excellency. The duke is *family*, after all."

"Ha! Yes, that's right. What else was it that you said to me? 'He'll never accept the invitation, Excellency. He wouldn't have the nerve to come back to Dullitch after the rat catastrophe.' Ha! Last time I listen to you! Tell him I'm busy."

"We did, my lord, and he attacked the guards."

"I beg your pardon?"

Spires fiddled nervously with his sleeves. "We told him you were busy and he tried to force his way in, then he punched young Halvn and ran away, so we gave chase. Halvn caught up with him, but the duke's, er, *bodyguard* gave the boy a damn good hiding."

"Hmm . . . rough sort, is he?"

"*She*, Excellency."

"Oh, for goodness' sa—"

"Exactly! Then they both ran away again.

Fortunately, one of our boys saw them go into a toy shop on Royal Road, so we got a squad together and arrested them."

"I see. Anything else?"

Spires nodded. "We also found the duke's manservant. He was up a tree at the corner of Palace 'n' Royal, Excellency."

Curfew put his head in his hands, and for a long time, the secretary thought he'd fallen asleep. Eventually, one eye opened.

"Show him in."

"And his staff, Excellency?"

"No, just Modeset. Lock the others up."

"Yes, Excellency." Spires reached for the door and stopped, his fingers hovering inches from the brass handle. "Should I, um, should I confiscate the items we found on him?"

"Hmm?"

"He was carrying a teddy bear and a small dolly, Excellency. When our men approached him, he brandished the latter as a weapon, claiming it could excrete acid. He was still fiddling with one of the legs when we managed to put the irons on him."

"Very well; confiscate his toys and *then* show him in."

"As you wish, Excellency."

The secretary bowed low and scurried from the room.

Moments later, he returned with the duke in tow.

TWELVE

CURFEW PACED back and forth before an immense circular window that commanded spectacular views of the cityscape, his lips twisted in a grim smile.

"Hmm . . . let us see what we have here: harassment of the palace guard, assault on an elf in the same occupation, two cases of evading the militia, and one of threatening behavior while brandishing a child's dolly. You have had a busy morning, cousin."

"Look," said Modeset, struggling against the weight of his chains. "If those imbeciles on the gate hadn't refused to admit me, none of the charges you just mentioned would exist!"

"Hmm . . . yes. If I were you, cousin, I'd take that tone of voice back to where it came from. I would remind you that you are now a guest here."

"What? Oh yes, right. Apologies." Modeset wasn't used to talking to anyone more important than himself; such people didn't exist within the boundaries of his own imagination.

"And, guesting," Curfew continued, "does require a certain amount of, how shall we say, host *tolerance*."

"Ha! That's a joke! You haven't even paid my bloody host!"

The viscount closed his eyes and clenched his fists tightly. "An oversight on my part, I confess," he said. "The matter will be rectified in time. As for your behavior—"

"I'll apologize to the guard I punched."

"Yes, you will," said Curfew moodily. "Also, you might think about keeping a low profile while you walk our busy streets. The people of Dullitch may have forgotten the rat catastrophe, but I'm sure your face will bring all those wonderful memories flooding back." The viscount folded his arms and raised both eyebrows expectantly. "I think you should leave now, cousin," he said.

Modeset flinched as Curfew snapped his fingers. Two imperial militiamen were suddenly all over him like a plague, throwing off chains and unscrewing manacles. Their task completed, Modeset found himself hoisted into the air and frogmarched through the echoing halls of the palace.

When Modeset was back on firm ground, the elf guard came waddling over to greet him. "Well, looky here," he said. "If it isn't his Imperial Lordship."

Modeset straightened himself up.

The guard waited.

Modeset gritted his teeth.

The guard waited.

"Well?" he said eventually.

"What's that?" said the duke. "If you think I'm apologizing to you, the rumors about elf intelligence must be spot on."

The guard, although obviously angered, showed no sign of retaliation. "That's okay," it said. "You can have your staff back the second you decide to change your mind."

Before he could protest, Modeset was thrown backward out onto the seething streets of Dullitch.

THIRTEEN

HAVING WASTED twenty crowns failing miserably at striking up a conversation with a young priestess on sabbatical, Jimmy Quickstint had retired to the smoky depths of the Rotting Ferret, where he planned to drink himself toward slow oblivion.

In some ways, Jimmy was glad to be rid of the job. Digging graves had never really suited him. Of course, it had been his first proper job (and would probably be his last), but these days it mainly served as a prop, something to fall back on when all else failed. Once upon a time, way back when, he'd been a thief; and even though he'd never really excelled, it was still the job he felt most proud of. He'd had some great times among the rooftop elite, and made some good friends along the way. Then, just after the terrible rat catastrophe, they'd kicked him out. O-U-T. Not so much as a by-your-leave.

Well, five years had passed since that fateful day. At first he'd adapted quite well, busking by day and telling stories at night. Now *that* was a profession, wandering from inn to inn, scratching a few crowns whilst propped against a fireplace with half a dozen bleary-eyed drunks staring up at you. Then the market expanded, and suddenly people were fed up with hearing about the fiddler who trapped death in a sack or the baker's boy who beat the demons at poker. Children especially wanted violence, unprovoked and brutal, and if the elves didn't put the shoemaker through a third-floor window, the children just weren't interested. Worse still, Jimmy Quickstint had actually found himself starting to adapt some of the old classics for this new bloodthirst. Snow White wasn't merely a pale princess, she was a Yowler assassin with vampiric tendencies; Little Red Riding Hood hadn't had any trouble with wolves since the day she acquired her grandmother's war hammer; and, once they'd encountered Goldilocks, the three bears had absolutely no intention of ever going home again.

The whole profession had quickly developed into

a battle between storytellers who'd begun to devise increasingly malevolent tales to entertain their audiences. Jimmy'd got out just before the well ran dry.

And here he was, a number of disastrous endeavors later.

Jobless.

He yawned and gazed down at the empty parchment he'd filched from the bar. As he suspected, the free quills handed out as samples by Counterfeit House weren't particularly good. He was just coming to grips with them, moving each one ghostlike over the crusty surface of the parchment, when his labors were interrupted.

"Mind if I join you?" said a familiar voice.

Jimmy looked up into the weathered face of Grab Dafisful, famed thief and Ferret regular during those murky hours between sunset and dawn. A lean man with a faint beard and extensive scarring, Grab was heavily rumored to be one of the only thieves in the city worth forking out for.

"Don't s'pose I can stop you," said Jimmy miserably. "But don't expect joviality."

"I expect nothing from a fellow thief except sympathy and friendly conversation," said Grab, pulling up a stool and peering at Jimmy's scrubby parchment with interest. "I 'aven't seen you for an age! What're you up to these days?"

"Not much," Jimmy snapped. "And I'm a grave-digger; haven't been a thief since Granddad died."

"It's quiet in 'ere tonight. 'ow's your grand-dad?"

Jimmy looked up quickly and was about to give the thief a piece of his mind when he remembered Grab's bizarre tendency not to listen to anything unless he was being looked directly in the eye. It was a disconcerting habit, and one very good reason why the man didn't have any friends.

"Granddad's dead," Jimmy reflected, uncomfortably staring the thief down. "He went years ago, just after the whole rat episode. And I'm not a thief anymore. Now I dig holes for dead people."

"I'm sorry."

"About what? My granddad or the job?"

"Both."

"Fine; sympathy accepted. Now, can I get on with writing this, please? It doesn't seem to be possible for me to continue this conversation and do some-thing else at the same time."

"Eh? 'ow d'you mean?"

"Never mind."

Jimmy sighed and returned his attention to the parchment, while Grab ordered two flagons of ale.

At length, the silence was broken.

"Out with it, then," Jimmy said, screwing up the parchment and tossing it across the floor. He leaned backward, forcing his chair onto two legs. "You never pay for a drink unless you're after something, so I might as well hear the pitch."

Grab managed to look hurt for all of fifty seconds before his face cracked into a smile. "All right," he said. "I need a favor. I've got myself into a bit of bother, as it 'appens."

"There's a surprise."

"No, I'm serious. Listen: last week I took on a job worth three 'undred."

"Crowns?" Jimmy's smile stayed exactly where it was, but the rest of his face sagged noticeably. "How come I never got offered jobs like that when I was a thief?"

"Trust me," Grab whispered conspiratorially. "The risk matched the reward."

"Oh?"

"Yeah. I 'ad to go up to Grinswood."

"What? That's at the other end of the continent!"

"Exac'ly. Then I 'ad to sneak through the deepest part of the forest and steal these baby lizards what can turn a man to stone if he isn't proper careful."

Jimmy scratched his chin. "Hmm . . . are you making this up?"

"No, I swear."

"Well, even with all that danger, three 'undred crowns is a pretty big fee. I mean, even after deductions there must be—"

"No deductions. Three 'undred straight."

Again, Jimmy's smile froze. "The Rooftop Runners *always* pay a percentage to the Yowlers," he said. "After all, one's a part of the other."

"Yeah, well, I know *that*, but this time it was different. This time I was workin' for the Yowlers themselves. It was 'ush-'ush an all. They came and got me in the night, took me to this church, and told me what I 'ad to do. Five of 'em, there were. Dead creepy an' all. I reckon most of the Yowlers don't even know 'bout it. I didn't see any o' the leaders there."

Jimmy suddenly felt a deep chill in his spine. "Are we getting to the bit where you need my help?" he asked uneasily.

Grab nodded.

"So," he continued, "I'm in this forest. I've

done the job, and I'm on my way out. Then, just as I'm stopping for a gasp o' air, this bird lands on a tree branch."

"Great gods." Jimmy yawned. "How much detail are we going into here?"

"Hang about; so this bird looks at me as if it knows what I done. Then off I go, outta the forest, and I stops the night at this village inn 'bout three miles south o' the forest, an' there it is, perched on the windowsill! The bird! And in the next village too! And now I'm back in Dullitch, and the bloody thing's still out there! Hunting me down!"

"Is that it? A bird?" Jimmy asked, dumbfounded. "Just ignore it."

"I can't! What if it's waitin' to see where I'm takin' the sack? It might be a spy, workin' for the viscount or even the Yowler leaders!"

Jimmy shook his head. "I don't think Viscount Curfew has many spies in the Grinswood."

"Well, that's as may be, but I don't want anything to go wrong with this job. If I make a mistake, lead an enemy to the door, so to speak, then bang goes my three 'undred crowns. Now, if you was to—"

"Stop right there," Jimmy interrupted. "I think I can see where this is going, and there's no way—"

"If we was to change clothes—"

"Not a chance."

"And I unscrewed my mechanical arm—"

"No, I said. No."

"Then you could put your 'ead down and run for it. By the time the bird saw that you weren't me, I'd have delivered my sack an' I'd be two 'undred and twenty-five crowns richer."

Jimmy waited a moment while he worked this out. "Let me get this straight: you're prepared to give me seventy-five crowns for impersonating you for an hour?"

"Yeah."

"To get away from a bird."

"'Sright."

"You're insane. I'll do it." He finished his ale and watched as Grab unscrewed his false limb. "Where is this bird, anyway?"

"Up the street." Grab pointed toward the Ferret's staircase. "It's perched on the sign over the Burrow Street Bakery, waitin' for me to come out. I'm convinced of it."

"Yeah, yeah. We'll see. Can we at least find a quiet spot to change clothes? I don't fancy exhibiting my valuables in front of this crowd."

FOURTEEN

JIMMY QUICKSTINT WAS having a really bad night. Apart from avoiding the barrowbird, his luck was such that he'd nearly walked straight into it. The situation called for all of his speed and cunning, so it was rather unfortunate that he didn't possess a great deal of either.

Then, to make matters worse, he'd dropped Grab's mechanical arm in Winding Way, and he had to stoop to pick it up, all the while trying to keep his face down and maintain his friend's insane half limp. It wasn't easy.

Finally, when he was at least six streets away from the Ferret and the crowds had begun to thicken, Jimmy spotted a convenient alleyway. Taking a deep breath and steeling all the muscles in his legs, he darted left, right, left, backward, forward, did a somersault, and then nose-dived behind a pile of rubbish sacks just beyond the mouth of the alley. There, squatting in the shadows, he waited for the bird to fly past.

It didn't.

Time passed, and there was still no sign of the creature.

The Diamond Clock on Crest Hill struck eleven and, motionless, Jimmy waited.

Eventually tiring of his awkward crouch, the gravedigger struggled to his feet and peered out into the street.

"Who're we lookin' for?" said a voice.

Jimmy turned and stared into the scruffy beak of the barrowbird. It had perched on a low wall opposite Jimmy's hiding place, and he was sure it was looking at him with malice.

"Game's up, genius," it squawked. "Worked like a treat; well done. Now stop soddin' about and tell me where your friend's gone."

"Wh-what? What friend? I don't have any friends."

"Don't mess with me, boy. You've no idea what you're getting involved in. I'm a magical bird, I am."

"Oh." Jimmy nodded. "Then I expect you can find him yourself."

There was an uncomfortable pause.

"I'll ask you once more, then I'll have your eyes out."

Jimmy looked nervously about, noticing on the edge of his vision that the gambling pits were opening for business.

"You don't look very fast," he said to the bird, edging carefully toward the alley mouth. "I could probably outrun you."

The bird hopped along the wall. "Try it," came the squawk.

"I might, at that," Jimmy said, and darted off across the road. The bird took flight and flapped speedily after him. The chase had begun.

Jimmy ran like lightning.

The bird flew like a bullet.

Jimmy slipped through the door of the inn.

The bird hit it.

"*Squawk! Squaark!* I'll get you yet, sonny. However long it takes, I'll be waiting. You'll rue the day you ever pulled the wool over my beak!"

The barrowbird flapped against the wood a few times, then flew up to sulk on the swinging sign of a nearby tavern.

Just after three o'clock, two bouncers carried out the comatose figure of a young man, dumping it unceremoniously in the alley across the street.

Before they disappeared back inside the murky depths of their pit, one of the bouncers was sure that he heard a menacing and somehow *feathery* cackle.

FIFTEEN

KARUIM'S CHURCH WAS unique in that it was the only building on Oval Square to have its entrance on Bark Street. Well, unique was perhaps too strong a word. After all, the buildings that occupied the other side of the square would've been hard-pressed to have their entrances on Bark Street without some sort of magic door in use. Nevertheless, Karuim's spurned the palace which dominated Oval Square, and many took this to be indicative of the Yowlers' notorious defiance in the face of royalty. Not that the church was wholly Yowler-run: it hadn't been so since a breakaway faction had claimed it a little more than a year ago.

The church itself was an eyesore, black as pitch and thoroughly shapeless, with an ugly gaping hole where its doors should have been. Worshippers

walked into this cave mouth and through the ensu-
ing tunnel system before emerging into the dark
expanse of the sanctuary proper.

It was a frightening journey, especially for Grab
Dafisful, who was increasingly of the opinion that
his every move was being watched, and not by a bird.
In fact, he couldn't help but feel, as he was about to
deliver his sack to the church's vestry, that the kind
of eyes currently monitoring his progress were the
sort that traveled back and forth to a belt dagger
between glimpses. Sweat beading on his forehead,
Grab reached for his own blade.

"Hmm . . . I'd move that hand back pretty
sharpish if I were you, especially since you've got
only the one."

Grab froze; the voice had come from behind
him. His hand hovered an inch or so above his belt.

"Throw down the knife," the voice commanded.
"You shouldn't bring such things into a house of the
gods."

The dagger clanked onto the stone floor, followed by three smaller blades and a set of knuckle-
dusters.

"Well, well, well," the voice continued. "You do
come prepared, Mr. Dafisful. Now, please deposit

your burden into the pew at your extreme left. Very good. Now, face front and prepare to answer a few questions."

While Grab did as he was told, a hand snaked around from behind him and snatched up the sack.

"Where's my money?" he shouted, being careful not to move a muscle.

"All in good time," said the voice. "First, the questions."

There followed some sort of commotion in the shadows before Grab noticed two cloaked shapes moving up the aisles on either side of him. Once in the center of the sanctuary, they separated, to stand not more than six feet apart. When given occasion to speak, they spoke together, more, Grab fancied, to disguise their individual voices than to create an air of mystery. It worked; the only thing he could be sure of was that one was male, the other female.

"Thief Dafisful. You have done as the brotherhood commanded?"

Grab nodded. "I 'ave."

"You have retrieved no less than ten Batchtiki from the Grinswood?"

"I have."

"You were not followed?"

"What? Er . . . not exactly, no."

A male voice this time, solo. "What do you mean by 'not exactly'? Either you were followed, or you were not."

Grab's movements became very fidgety. "There *was* this bird, you see, and—"

"A bird?"

"Yeah, and I thought it was—"

"As in 'flap flap' bird?"

"Er . . . yes."

The female voice took up the questioning. "We have no interest in birds. When we asked if you were followed, we were talking beast, not bird."

Grab's features creased like a brown paper bag. "No, I'm sure I wasn't followed by any of them."

"Good. And you spoke of your endeavors to no one?"

"Nope. Definitely not. No, siree. I'm not stupid, me. I spoke to no one. Well, no one worth speaking of . . ."

"So, in fact, you *did* tell somebody."

"Um . . . sort of. Yeah."

There was a collective sigh. "More than one person?"

"No. Just the one, I swear. Just Jimmy. 'e's a friend of mine, ex-thief, understands perfectly. 'e won't tell a soul."

"Hmm . . . we shall see. For now, you may go."

" 'ey! What about my money?"

"You will find it beside the decorative font on your way out."

Grab nodded and turned to leave, muttering to himself about conspiracies and the kind of people who lurked in shadows. He didn't see a soul on his way out of the church, but, even as he collected his money, he felt they were watching him. In the shadows.

As soon as Grab had left the sanctuary, two dark hoods were drawn back in unison.

"Your thief talks too much," said the female voice. "He'll have to be silenced."

"And his friend?" echoed her male counterpart. "This Jimmy? A danger, you think?"

"Undoubtedly."

"We can't just leave it and hope. We're too near!"

"Exactly."

"Two jobs for Mixer, then?"

"Ha! If our little gnome's as good as you say he is, Lopsalm, I'm sure he's dealing with it already. . . ."

"Oh, he is, my dear. I can assure you of that."

"He'll need to be fast, mind; thieves like Grab can be wily and resourceful."

Lopsalm turned in the darkness.

"A good job we dispatched Moors and Edwy, then, isn't it?"

SIXTEEN

GRAB HAD A terrible feeling in the pit of his stomach. Keeping a tight grip on the money pouch with his remaining hand, he began to run.

Footsteps echoed behind him.

On he ran, urging his tired body through the pain barrier.

The footsteps increased with him, and he heard the distinctive sound of a crossbow being primed.

Grab peered over his shoulder, caught the merest glimpse of a small figure as it nipped into a doorway, and then he started to run, very fast.

The streets, slippery and lashed with rain, were deserted; they seemed to flitter past as Grab hurtled around corners and leaped over bins in a frantic dash for the safety of the market square. He knew the stalls would be long gone, but there were *always* people in the square. There *had* to be.

Incredibly, the rainstorm picked up. Grab thought he saw a shape up ahead; large, almost impossibly so. Was it a troll or a person? Difficult to tell. Grab strained to see through the veil of rain. Yes, a person. Definitely. Thank the gods. Now, if he could just put on another burst of speed . . .

The shape lumbered forward, and Grab almost fell into it.

"Hey, watch it."

"I'm sorry," Grab managed, righting himself and standing back to stare in awe at the size of the human mass before him. "There's someone after me. . . ."

"I can't see anybody."

Grab swung around and squinted into the rain. "No, well. I could swear I was being followed." He turned back. "Anyway, it's a nice nigh—"

The lumbering shape threw out a fist so hard that Grab almost achieved flight as he fell backward, landing in the middle of a collection of rubbish bins with a resounding crash.

The rain hammered down. As Grab fought to get to his feet, he noticed that his noisy collision with the rubbish had failed to attract even the slight-est hint of attention; not a light in a window, not the creak of a door. Grab moaned as he regained his footing.

Shapes loomed up ahead; the large man who'd hit him had now been joined by a second, slimmer figure. Grab turned on his heels and started to run, hopelessly, back toward the church. After a few steps, he hesitated, then stopped and peered over his shoulder. The two men weren't moving; they were simply standing there, closing off the end of the street.

Grab tried to think clearly, his head still fuzzy from the strength of the big man's punch. They were obviously herding him toward a greater danger. He shook his head, then turned back and practically walked into the gnome.

Mixer was standing in the street, his brass teeth glinting in the glow of the streetlamp beside him. He was holding a large and very nasty-looking cross-bow.

Grab turned yet again, and ran. His hope was to break through the human barricade up ahead. He made a last, desperate dash.

Lightning split the sky, and thunder echoed

through the clouds. The rain came down hard . . .

. . . and so did Grab Dafisful.

"Ahhhh!"

The bolt struck home, spearing into the thief's back and forcing him forward. Grab gasped, his legs folded under him. Rain plastered his hair to his forehead. He laid a hand flat against the cobbles and tried to push himself up, but the gnome was on him.

Thunder boomed overhead, announcing its warning to any citizens who hadn't already turned their mirrors to face the wall.

"Ahhh! No! Mercy, I beg you!"

Mixer drove a boot into the small of the thief's back, reloaded the crossbow, and aimed it at his head. Then he pulled the trigger.

There was a sickening thud.

As the last of the rain came down, the corpse of Grab Dafisful was dragged into a nearby doorway and left propped up against the door like a stuffed dummy. Mixer smiled at his handiwork, and promptly departed.

PART TWO

THE

DUKE

AND THE

DETECTIVE

SEVENTEEN

ODESET WAS FUMING, and with good reason.

He'd been walking through the streets all night. He was dirty, hungry, and worst of all, he didn't have anyone else to blame. All he had were choices. He didn't want to go back to the Steeplejack Inn without the others (the innkeeper was enough of a pain as it was), and he certainly had no intention of loitering anywhere near the palace, so he'd decided to kick off his new day with a depressed stroll around the harbor district instead.

It wasn't a bad day, by Dullitch standards, and the sun glinted off the highly polished paintwork of *The Mostark*, the viscount's supreme galleon. Modeset wondered if he'd ever own such a ship again. Considering his current finances, a rowing boat seemed the more likely option, if they hired them out.

Heading along the quay, he came upon a small platform where two dwarfs were unloading a heavy crate of Legrash Ale. They tried to lift the crate, failed, and then proceeded to drag it off the platform, accompanied by an orchestra of grunts and groans. Modeset asked if he could lend a hand, expecting them to decline.

"You're on," said the older of the two, a dwarf with a beard almost down to his ankles. "Get at the side and guide us in."

Reluctantly, Modeset did as he was told. The dwarfs took a breath, lifted again, and set off, remarking on how the ale seemed even heavier than before. They were right, too; Modeset didn't like to admit it, but after the first few feet, they were actually carrying him as well. Some of these dockers, he reflected, had more sinews than sense.

At length, the crate was set down and the dwarf with the beard consulted a tattered scroll fastened to the lid.

"I'm done believin' it," he said. "What kind of grizzled nut am I?"

His colleague waited for the bad news.

Modeset, sensing the possibility of further involvement, had already taken a step back.

"This is supposed to go on to Spittle," the first dwarf said.

"So?" said the other docker moodily.

"So, it's the Day of Storms, right? Day of Storms cargo for Spittle. See any connection there? We should be in Warehouse Five, not Warehouse Six. Let's move it out. C'mon."

The second dwarf prepared to lift the crate, then stopped and looked about.

"Where's the bloke who was helpin' us?" he said.

"Dunno," said the first. "Maybe he fell under the crate."

They burst into a roaring, gut-rooted laughter and, after four attempts, carried the crate over to Warehouse Five.

Meanwhile, Modeset hunkered down in the shadows. Either through fate or fortune, he'd found himself in the warehouse that the scroll had mentioned. What harm could it do to take a look around?

Apart from an aging hill troll unpacking barrels in the northwest corner, the warehouse was deserted. Crates of various shapes and sizes, piled haphazardly with barely an inch between stacks, reached almost to the rafters in every direction. The trick, he decided, was to know where to start in such a maze of merchandise.

Stay away from Warehouse Six. The words rang in his ears, but they offered no clue. Still, he suspected he'd recognize something to stay well away from as soon as he got on top of it.

Time passed.

Modeset squeezed between row upon row of crates, studying the little scrolls attached to each one.

As it turned out, the cargo came from all over Illmoor and included unmarked stock from Legrash, Spittle, the Gleaming Mountains, the Twelve, Shadewell, Carafat, Grinswood, and Sporring.

More time passed.

Modeset stalked the aisles. It was beginning to dawn on him that there was a lot more to this investigating lark than met the eye, when a voice interrupted his train of thought.

"S'cuse me," it said. "This is private prop'ty and you're a trusspisser."

Modeset had his answer all worked out.

Unfortunately, when he turned around to supply it, the troll head-butted him.

As a red mist drifted over Modeset's field of vision, his hulking attacker stomped off to look for a crate winch.

EIGHTEEN

ELSEWHERE, MORNING found Mixer in a quiet corner of Mudsen Mill, the city's premier café. When the stout (but not unpleasant-looking) waitress had delivered two squares of charred toast, he peered around for any obvious signs of attention before producing a tattered notebook from the recesses of his jerkin.

Flipping open the top leaf, he ran a grubby finger down the hastily scribbled list of names. Then, plucking a tiny length of lead from behind his ear, he put a neat line through the last two.

That was the inventor *and* the thief out of the way. Now there were only a few loose ends to worry about.

He studied the remaining list and considered his options. As far as he could see, there was one "urgent" and a possible "pending."

The loftwing wouldn't wait much longer. In fact, Mixer had already decided that the next time he was followed, the investigator would get what was coming to him, indubitably. Then there was the boy: Dafisful *had* spent a long time talking to the young wastrel in the Ferret. He might have told him anything; hell, he might have told him *everything*. So: another one to add to the list. If only there were a little more time! Still, needs must . . .

First things first, he told himself. Breakfast—the most important meal of the day.

Mixer took one last glance at the notebook before returning it to his jerkin pocket. Then he ordered a coffee to go with his charcoal.

NINETEEN

JIMMY QUICKSTINT, half barefoot on the cold cobbles of the alley in which he'd spent the night, was livid. Of course, he'd enjoyed himself at first. Everybody did. This was because, for sheer incredible logic, gambling was hard to beat. You came in off the street with bugger-all except three acorns and a foot infection, and in less than fifteen minutes you had a bag of gold, six illegitimate children, and a couple of empty cottages in lower Dullitch with rental possibilities. That, of course, was if you were endowed with luck, knew how to play, and carried loaded dice.

Jimmy wasn't, didn't, and hadn't. He'd been carried from the pits of Primo Don barely three hours after he went in, having parted with two shoes, one sock, and his left eyebrow. The latter, he'd been assured, he could claim back at a later date in exchange for the seventeen crowns he owed Logoff the Merchant. Additionally, to form a nice creamy topping on his elephantine disaster of a day, he now found himself hungry and alone in a part of the city he had hitherto only seen on the secondhand maps outside the cartography school.

He was about to make a move, when a frighteningly familiar voice said: "You're up, then?"

Jimmy turned slowly on his heels and found himself staring into the beak of the barrowbird.

"Leave me *alone!*"

"Shan't."

"Damn you!"

"Nice."

"No, I mean it! Damn you to hell."

"Colorful; do you blaspheme professionally or are you still on the amateur circuit?"

Jimmy extended a finger to support his annoyance. "Stuff this in your beak and curse you, you emaciated feathered twit."

"Listen, you can damn me all you like. I told you last night that I wouldn't be easy to shake off."

"Yes, but what do you want?"

"Your friend with the limp."

"But I don't know where he is!"

"Then find him, and I'd be pretty sharpish if I were you. I'm not a patient bird."

Jimmy fell against the alley wall and allowed himself to slide down. "This is ridiculous!" he gasped. "Do you have any idea how big Dullitch is? He could be anywhere!"

"He's *your* friend. You must know where he hangs out."

Jimmy shook his head. "Thieves aren't like that," he said. "They only come to you when they need something, and I've already done Grab a favor, remember?"

The barrowbird flapped a bit, then appeared to reach a decision. "You'll have to go back to the tavern," it squawked.

Jimmy shrugged. "It's a long shot."

"Do you know any short ones?"

"No."

"Then get movin'!"

TWENTY

VISCOUNT CURFEW sighed deeply. "I take it you have some bad news, Spires?"

His royal secretary paused in the doorway, unsure of whether he should risk an entrance. "Wh-why do you say that, lord?"

"You only come to see me on such occasions."

"Oh, I . . ."

Curfew raised an eyebrow. "Well? Do go on."

"Um, right, er, the fact is, that, in fact, the point being . . ."

"Quickly, please. Before one of us dies."

"Yes, sir. Of course. What would you like first? The atrocious end of the news or its abysmal beginnings?"

"Start with the atrocious and work your way backward. That way you have at least a thirty percent chance of survival."

Spires closed the door to the chamber behind him and took a seat on the base of a marble plinth, clearing his throat in the process.

"A short while ago I fired one of the scribes, a young lady by the name of Lauris."

"On what grounds?"

"Um . . . the palace grounds, sir."

"No, you idiot, *what grounds did you have to fire her?*"

"Oh right, I see. Well, our people were watching her for some time, and I knew, at second hand, of at least three activities that she could have been fired for, but I actually *caught* her signing import orders."

"*Import orders?* For what?"

Spires scratched nervously at his arm. "Machinery, sir. Tin, iron; some enchanted bronze too, if I recall; all sorts of nonsense. Unfortunately, she burnt the paperwork shortly before we confronted her, and now we can't find out where she stored these . . . *supplies*. Wherever it was, they've probably been moved on by now."

"And the girl?"

"She disappeared, sir. The spies observed that several palace-stamped scrolls disappeared at around the same time."

"Why on earth wasn't she fired before?"

"Well, the fact is, Excellency, she did a lot of very positive things for us."

"Such as?"

"Well, um, trade deals and the like. In fact, it was Lauris who found out about your new statue and suggested that we have it moved down from Spittle to put in the cit— Why are you looking at me like that, Excellency?"

"Never mind. It just seems curious then that she made such a nuisance of herself. It doesn't really add up, does it?"

"No, Excellency. Not at all."

"And now she's probably up to something dodgy with our stamped scrolls, no doubt. What use would they be?"

The servant took a deep breath. "No use whatsoever *inside the city*, Excellency. As for foreign powers, well, I expect she could send a few bogus war declarations, but nothing any of the major cities would take seriously without a herald to back it up."

"So no threat there, then. How long since she vacated the palace?"

Spires fidgeted nervously on the little platform. "Approximately two weeks, give or take a day," he said.

Curfew shut his eyes for a moment, then opened

them again. "And you only thought to tell me about it now?"

"Um, I didn't want to alarm you, Excellency."

"Is that right? I'm assuming you've taken steps to find this girl?"

"Of course, Excellency. We hired an investigator to track her down; we thought it might be better to work quietly so as not to attract undue attention."

"Has he turned up anything?"

"Yes and no, Excellency, yes and no. He called at her house on North Street, aiming to search for some clue as to her whereabouts, but when he arrived, he found a gnome torching the place."

Curfew's expression twisted into the half smirk of the intrigued. "A gnome."

"Yes, Excellency, a gnome."

"And did he capture this gnome?"

"No, the report says that he made no attempt to do so. He suspected that if he followed this *gnome*, then maybe it would lead him to Lauris herself."

"Hmm . . . a fair conclusion, I suppose. Is that all?"

"No, milord. The whole thing has become quite a bit more complicated. Mr. Obegarde, that's the investigator, he's been asking questions up at City

Hall, and they say that this gnome is the caretaker at Karuim's."

Curfew's expression suddenly froze. "That's a Yowler building, isn't it?"

"Yes, Excellency, which is why I thought it best to tell you about all this in the first place. We might have a real problem, here."

"I see." The viscount rose from his chair and, marching over to the window, stared out at the steeples of the great church. "This girl, this . . . Lauris. You must talk to everyone in the palace who worked with her, Spires," he said. "Friends, enemies, rivals, I don't care who they are, I want a complete report of her history. We need to know if she has or had any connection with the Yowler Brotherhood. Leave no stone unturned!"

The secretary bowed low and hurriedly vacated the chamber, leaving the viscount to his thoughts.

TWENTY-ONE

MODESET AWOKE to find himself in a crate. His eyes ached, and drums beat a steady rhythm inside his head. He moaned, brought a hand to his chin, and wiped away a crusted mixture of blood and spittle.

I'm a duke, he thought. I'm royalty! They can't get away with treating me like this! I'm off to the palace, and Curfew will *have* to listen this time because I'm family and because I'm of the blood! Someone's going to have to pay; someone like that elf, someone who, someone . . . SOMEONE GET ME OUT OF THIS BLOODY CRATE!

He aimed both feet at the lid and kicked frantically, elbowing the sides for good measure. Just when he was beginning to make some headway, he heard the faintest hint of a whisper. At first, he thought it might be the wind, but then, ever so slightly, the volume increased.

"Stpt."

Modeset strained to listen.

"Opit—"

"What? Is someone out there?"

The next time the voice spoke, it was clearly audible. "Stop it," it said. "Stop wriggling. Don't move another inch."

"What do you mean, 'Don't move another inch'?" screamed Modeset. "Help! Get me out of here!"

"Quieten down!" said the voice, increasing in urgency. "The dockers are patrolling tonight and I can't handle all of 'em. Stay quiet and they'll pass."

"Tonight? You mean I've been in here all day? Damn that troll!"

"Shh! Listen, you don't know where you are."

Modeset fidgeted inside his prison. "Don't be ridiculous," he said. "I'm in a crate."

"Okay," the voice continued. "Let's put it another way. You don't know where the crate is."

There followed a few seconds of expectant silence.

"Why?" asked Modeset, voice quavering. "Where is it?"

"Roughly? About twenty-five feet off the ground. So stay still."

A brief scuffling ensued and Modeset suspected that he heard a rope being winched. There was a sharp creak, and suddenly he felt the crate move in the air. After a time, it swung left, leaving him with an empty feeling in the pit of his stomach. Then, slowly at first, it began to descend.

"Okay," said the voice. "Let's get this off."

The head of a crowbar bit into the wood and the lid of the crate was wrenched clear. Modeset pulled himself up and looked out at a dark shadow. His eyes traveled from shiny black boots to a thatch of jet-black hair that crowned the shadow in all its menacing glory. Recognition dawned very gradually.

"It's you! Why are you dressed like that?"

The loftwing looked down at himself. "I always dress like this," he said. "It's part and parcel of the job. If I don't dress like this, people won't recognize me. Now, may we dispense with the pleasantries?"

Modeset frowned and nodded, before a fist like bunched steel sent him careering back into the crate.

Obegarde stepped forward and pulled the duke up again. "I thought I told you to keep your nose out of this," he snapped, supporting Modeset by the base of his chin. "What is it with dukes? I've known a few, and you're all the same. You go gallivanting around on the merest whim, sticking your noses into every kind of trouble, as if the world owes you a favor. Well, if I remember rightly, Dullitch certainly doesn't owe you any favors."

Modeset wriggled free and shook his head. "It's not what you think," he said, still in shock and spitting blood with every second word. "I got here by accident."

"A likely story."

"No, it's true. This afternoon, after I got arrested—"

"You?" Obegarde's half-smile came as a definite relief. "How did you get arrested? Parked your carriage over a trade route or something?"

"I punched a guard," Modeset managed.

"Really? I'm impressed, but that still doesn't explain what you're doing here. . . ."

"Yes, well—"

"And you've only got five minutes until I lose my famous kind streak."

The duke tried to explain.

Obegarde pretended to listen.

"Well," Obegarde said, when Modeset had brought his tale up to date. "Now you're here, you might as well see what it is our friend doesn't want me to find."

He took a step back and gestured behind him.

Modeset squinted into the darkness and shrugged. "I don't see anything."

"You sure?"

"Of course I'm sure! There's nothing there! I know because that's the way I came in. If there was a crate standing on its own, I'd have seen it."

Obegarde's grin stayed right where it was. "It's not a crate," he said. "Look again."

Modeset stared hard at the wall of the warehouse, except that it wasn't the wall of the warehouse. It was the back of something. Something huge.

"Ye gods!" he cried. "What is it? It's enormous."

"You're telling me," said Obegarde, scratching his granite forehead.

"I must have walked right past it!"

"So did I, three times. For some reason, you just can't comprehend it at first."

"But what in the name of the gods is it?"

The loftwing shrugged. "A machine of some kind," he said. "It's camouflaged to blend in with the warehouse wall. The Harbor Master's an elf, so there's no way he doesn't know about it . . . which leads me to believe that the owner of this monster holds sway over at least one high-ranking member of the Mariners' Consortium."

"It's glowing," remarked Modeset, taking a step back.

"Yeah, it does seem to do that, on and off," said Obegarde. "At a guess, I'd say it's part magic and part machine. There's a lens on the top, a lever on the side, and tubes all over the pace. It's got me puzzled, I don't mind admitting."

Modeset narrowed his eyes. "I don't like the look of it," he said. "There's something inherently destructive in the shape. Who do you think owns it? Your rock-thrower?"

"Could be, could be," said Obegarde, nodding. "He visits it every night. That's what first led me here. And he always brings a book. Does nothing with it, mind. It's almost as if he just brings the thing so he doesn't have to leave it at home."

Modeset nodded. "Odd. Well, um, how am I going to get out of here, exactly?"

The investigator grinned. "You're not," he said. "You're gonna come with me while I break into the

Harbor Master's office. I need to see if there's any record of this monstrosity in the holding log."

The first kick wrenched the cottage door from its hinges, the second sent it crashing to the floor.

"I thought you said the dockers were watching this place," Modeset whispered.

"They are," said Obegarde with a shrug. "That's why I knew we wouldn't have any trouble getting in."

"I'm sorry I—"

"Dockers generally aren't too bright. They're big and slabby, but not too quick on the brain trigger."

The Dullitch Harbor Master's office was a bit of a dump; Modeset couldn't see for anchors.

"Here we are," called Obegarde, clambering over the desk to study the heavy logbook. "Hmm, recent entries . . . Aha!"

Modeset kept watch, peering around the fractured door like a nervous whippet.

"Interesting," said the investigator, scratching his concrete chin.

"What? What is it?"

"Well, you need two signatures to legally deposit a crate, especially when it's unlikely to leave the city. The machine is logged in as Herman's Stare.

There's a brief disclosure note signed by one Augustus Vrunak, address in upper Dullitch. The other signature's too blurry to make out, but the address is definitely Karuim's."

"The church next to the palace?" Modeset asked.

"Hmm . . . my last stop, I think. Night's almost over." He looked up and saw Modeset backing out the door. "Hey! Where're you going?"

"Home!" said the duke. "And it's no use you trying to stop me; I'm tired and I want to get some sleep."

Obegarde rolled his eyes. "You're joking, right?" he said. "Besides, I need some help here; you might as well just come with me. We'll both head back to the Steeplejack when we're done."

"No!" Modeset shook his head. "I'm off *now*. None of this has anything to do with me. *You* can go wherever you like."

"Okay, okay" said the investigator. "But you *are* involved now, whether you like it or not, so can you at least do me a favor?"

The duke sighed. "That depends; what kind of favor? Does it involve me dressing up, spending time in a confined space, or becoming embroiled in a street fight?"

"No." Obegarde shook his head and passed him a small square of paper torn from the logbook. "Check out this Vrunak fellow for me."

"What, now?"

"Not necessarily. Get your precious sleep; you can go tomorrow morning. Here's the address."

Modeset was about to decline, but when he saw the look on the loftwing's rugged face, he thought better of it.

TWENTY-TWO

THE ROTTING FERRET was bustling with activity. Chas Firebrand's decision to sell the subterranean inn to a family of goblins from Phlegm had seemed a disastrous one on paper, but Frowd Fjin was certainly a greenskin with talent. In a little over five years, he'd turned the place from an oft-avoided fighting pit into a respected nightclub, complete with orc bouncers, elf waitresses, and even a troglodyte cabaret group.

Jimmy was miserable; he'd been waiting at the inn for hours, and there was not even the merest hint of a sign of Grab Dafisful. Worse still, he knew that the barrowbird was waiting outside and, no matter how many ingenious ways he might invent to leave the Ferret, his feathered curse would eventually catch up with him.

"So, let me get this straight," he muttered to the gnome, who'd taken a seat beside him and promptly ordered a round. "You're saying that you can smash the green bottle above the bar, third along on the right, without anyone knowing it was you? Get out."

Mixer waved him into silence. "A crown says I can, a drink says I can't."

"Done."

The gnome then quickly produced a small but intricate-looking crossbow, then lowered his head and fired off a shot, thrusting the weapon under the table before the merest hint of breaking glass.

"Oi!" bellowed the landlord, a swarthy half-ogre. "Who did that? We'll have no such sport in 'ere!"

Jimmy turned, mouth still agape, to stare at the gnome. "Drinks're on me, then," he said. "Incredible. Just incredible."

Mixer shrugged. "You think that's impressive ?" he started, drawing closer to the gravedigger and lowering his voice to a conspiratorial whisper. "I can make the bells of Karuim's toll without even touching them."

"Rubbish; now that *is* impossible."

"Ha! That's what Grab said this morning. He's laughing on the other side of his face now!"

"Grab? Not Grab Dafisful, the thief?"

"Yeah, the very same. Why, d'you know him?"

"Know him? He . . . er . . . he owes me fifty crowns!"

Mixer's tiny eyes lit up. "Oh, it's you he owes!" The gnome tapped at his shiny brass teeth. "He said as much; just between us, he's hiding up on the roof of Karuim's Church. I met him this morning when I was doing some routine maintenance work for the council. In fact, I'm due back there in a minute. D'you fancy joining me? You can have a word with Grab and then we can see who takes this incredibly fine piece of weaponry home. What d'you say?"

Jimmy, ever the sucker for a gamble, took the proffered weapon in his hands and looked it over. It was made of Chakiwood, the poisoned bark of the Red Lime Tree. Rare; expensive. It had to be worth at least a hundred crowns.

"You're on," Jimmy agreed, passing the cross-bow back to the gnome with a nod.

"We'll call it a deal, then," said Mixer, staring dispassionately at the barmaid as she delivered their long-awaited tankards of ale. "Unless you want to start small; I can't imagine a fellow like you has too much gold."

Jimmy tried to keep a straight face, which was difficult with a mug like his. One thing everyone in the city knew about Jimmy, apart from the fact that he used to be a thief and was reasonably good with a shovel, was his marked annoyance at anyone suggesting that he was penniless.

He raised one eyebrow and tried to focus on the Rotting Ferret's rowdy clientele.

"I'm doing okay, as a matter of fact," he lied. "So let's talk turkey; when do you want me to witness your terrible failure at the church? Now?"

A silence settled over the table.

"Well, there's no time like the present. Isn't that what they say?"

"Sure, okay. Give me a minute to pay the piper; I'll be right back."

"Awesome," Mixer said, with an evil grin. "Hurry up, though. I can't hang around all night."

Jimmy nodded, jumped out of his chair, and dashed through the bar. Once safely beyond the grimy door that led to the Ferret's condemned latrines, he hurtled along a dank passage, up three flights of half-crumbled steps, past a dingy back door, over the wall in the Ferret's beer garden, down the alley that clung to its western side, and out into the street that contained the inn's decrepit entrance doors.

The barrowbird spotted him immediately, alighting from its perch on a first-floor windowsill of a bakery across the road.

"Anything?" it squawked. "I haven't seen him go in."

"He's not there," Jimmy hurriedly confided. "But I'm talking to a gnome who's gonna take me to him."

"A gnome?"

"Yeah."

"What, just like that?"

"Yes!"

"No questions asked?"

"Yes, I mean, no!"

"Does the gnome know anything about the group that hired him?"

"I don't know!"

"Can't you find out?"

"NO!"

"Why not?"

"Look, it's simple. He thinks he owes me money!"

"Who, the gnome?"

"Grab, damn it! Why don't you listen?"

"I am listening; why can't you speak properly?"

"Don't start with me! I'm doing you a favor here."

"Ha! You dug your own grave, boy. Now *you* listen. Why don't you follow this dwarf—"

"It's a gnome, and I'm going to!"

"Right, and then I'll follow the pair of you."

"D'you think so? Gad, and I thought I was sharp. Can I go now?"

"No, wait! Just hang on a minute; how did you get out?"

"I lied; told him I was going to the latrine."

"Right. So hadn't you better get back inside then, so we can follow him when he leaves?"

"Yes! That's what I'm saying!"

"Well, don't let me keep you."

Jimmy rolled his eyes. Then he raced back down the alley, leaped over the wall, shouldered past the door, fell down the stairs, hurtled along the corridor, bumped his way through the bar, landed on the three-legged stool opposite the gnome, and promptly fell off it.

Mixer swallowed a gulp of ale.

"That was quick," he said.

TWENTY-THREE

IGHT YAWNED. . . .

When Modeset returned to the Steeplejack Inn, he found Flicka waiting for him.

The duke had always had a curious relationship with the girl, partly because he found her very beautiful, but mostly because he didn't feel at all comfortable with young women. Any women, come to that.

However, observing her now as she stood in the entrance hall of the inn, with her hair plastered to her face and her ragged clothes heavy with rain, Modeset was beginning to understand what all the fuss was about. The girl was healthy, that much was certain.

"Well, I say, what a surprise," he began. "I was very, very worried about you, Flicka. In fact, I was just this minute coming to get you out of the dungeons and, whoosh-adacadava, here you are. Most impressive."

Flicka raised a thick eyebrow. Her brown eyes glistened. "On your way to getting us out?" she said. "How thoughtful, milord. Odd, though, I seem to recall the palace being in the opposite direction."

Modeset nodded quickly. "Yes, well of course it *is*," he said. "But I was planning to get some shut-eye first, you know, conserve a bit of energy."

"That's fine," said Flicka, beaming. "I'll grab the carriage from the stables and you can get some rest on the way to the guardhouse."

"The guardhouse?"

"Yes. They've still got Pegrand, and they won't let him out until you apologize to the guard. They only let me out because I'm a woman."

She swept back her hair with both hands, bunched up two fistfuls of it, and secured the resulting locks with a length of twine. Then, still grinning, she took a step toward the door.

Modeset held up a hand. "We're not going to the palace," he said. His tone was set in lead.

"What? But you said you were—"

"It's not done for a duke to apologize, and

besides, that guard had it coming. All elves are deviants."

"That's a rotten attitude for a duke, especially here. It's not right to persecute any of Mother Nature's children."

"Not right? You can't rely on Mother Nature, you know. Just look at what she did to Pegrand. Besides, we don't have time for this nonsense, or to mess about rescuing people. I need some sleep and so do you."

Flicka looked suddenly wretched. "What about Pegrand?" she said.

"I'll get him out in the morning," said Modeset, after a pause.

"You promise?"

"Yes. Now go!"

He watched her turn and make for the stairs, listening for any hint of a giggle. He was about to retire himself, when the innkeeper came barrelling out of the dining hall.

"Bloody nuisance," he spat. "Shutters broken. More bloody money."

"Yes," said the duke. "I'm terribly sorry if that puts you out."

"Puts me out, you say? Puts me out? You're a nuisance."

"Yes, again, my apologies. Any chance of a new room tonight?"

"Any chance? No chance. Sleep in the alley, far as I'm concerned. You're a bloody curse, the lot o' you."

Modeset shot forward. The movement was sudden and unexpected, and the innkeeper found himself pinned against the hall wall.

"Now listen up," snapped the duke. "I've told you you'll see your money, so get this straight; you'll give me a new room, a better room with a nice soft bed and a proper window; you'll stop moaning; you'll be pleasant to my staff; and if I get even the slightest hint that you've been spitting in the wine, they'll find you where I leave you. Now, do we have an understanding?"

The innkeeper swallowed, and Modeset thought he could just make out a nod.

TWENTY-FOUR

DULLITCH WAS A CITY full of filth and, as Obegarde could testify, it all floated to the surface at downtime.

Downtime. He repeated the word over and over, working it into a steady rhythm. His boots splashed water as they hit the puddle-strewn cobbles.

Downtime was the affectionately named period between midnight and sunup when some of Dullitch's darkest, weirdest, and most nocturnally bound citizens began to stir. It was also a time in which the city had a strangely isolated air; the streets were shadowy, lamplight was bleak, and, nine times out of ten, it was pissing rain in the bargain. Downtime was the only time certain people could walk the streets.

People like Obegarde.

The wind whistled, rolling bottles along the damp cobbles and turning over rubbish bins across the city.

On the roof of Karuim's Church, an ancient, rust-riddled weather vane moaned in the wind, broke from its support, and fell. It landed three inches short of Obegarde.

The investigator flinched. His hearing went fuzzy. A breeze ruffled the flaps of his dark coat. He looked behind him.

Embedded deep in the cobbles, the weather vane was still taller than a man, its base jutting out of the earth like the hilt of a giant's dagger. A few twisted brackets hung loose. The metal finger that acted as the vane's indicator had folded back on itself. Obegarde noticed, with some small degree of amusement, that it now pointed skyward.

The entrance to the church flew open, and a man came hobbling up a stone flight of stairs that ascended from the tunnel below. He was elderly, awkward, and bespectacled. He wore a ragged suit of leather.

Obegarde squinted through the rain. "Nasty night," he said, when the old man was within earshot. He nodded down at the fractured weather vane. "Narrow escape, there. I was lucky."

The stranger's scowl suggested that "lucky" would have meant that Obegarde had been underneath the vane when it fell.

Obegarde extended his hand, waited for about a minute, and then withdrew it.

"Good evening," he began, his mind racing for a suitable ruse. "I've come about thejdjffkfkdk."

"What?"

"I've said I've come about thejdjjfjdfjfj."

"I can't hear you. Speak up!"

"Can I come in?"

The old man hobbled up to him and, to Obegarde's extreme surprise, actually stepped on his toes. When he spoke, uncomfortably close, his breath smelled like rotting flesh.

"Eh? What's that?"

"The church! Can I come into the church?"

"I wouldn't advise it."

"Why?"

"There's nobody there."

"Oh. Nobody at all?"

The church acolyte cocked his head to one side and gave Obegarde a critical stare, practically from inside his own eyeballs.

"You could always talk to Lopsalm," he said eventually. "Lopsalm's inside."

"I thought you said there was nobody inside."

"Yes, yes, but Lopsalm doesn't count. He's mad, you see. Quite, quite mad. It's *your* funeral."

Obegarde shoved the old man backward, then took a step forward himself.

"Lopsalm it is," he said, pushing past. "Thanks for your help."

TWENTY-FIVE

"**W**ELL," JIMMY SAID, looking around the haunted expanse of the church roof. "Where's Grab? I don't see him anywhere."

Mixer put an experimental foot to the nearest gargoyle and leaned forward. Then he turned to Jimmy and gave a shrug. "Who knows? Maybe he took off."

"Um . . . right."

"Thieves are like that, aren't they? Unreliable, I mean."

"I wasn't."

"You? You were a thief?"

"Yeah, a while ago now, but I was never very good at it. Not like Grab; he's one of the best."

Mixer nodded. "I'm sure he wa . . . I mean *is*."

"Right. I wonder where he went."

"Hmm . . . a mystery."

"Yeah." Jimmy wandered across to the edge of the church. "Cold up here, isn't it?" he ventured, squinting at the gravestones far below. He shivered and shook his head. "Long way down."

He started to head over to the small tower containing the church's gargantuan brass bell.

"Well?" he said. "Let's see this thing chime, then."

"Indeed," came the reply. Mixer grinned. "It'll chime like never before."

"Without you touching it, o' course," Jimmy added.

"Of course. Here goes. . . ."

The gnome raised his crossbow and leveled it.

"Ah . . . of course; I should've guessed. You're gonna shoot it, eh?"

Jimmy took a step back.

"No! Stay exactly where you are," Mixer snapped.

"What? But I'm in the way!"

"Yes, you *are* . . . and so was Grab Dafisful. He had to die too."

"What? What are you talking about?"

Mixer's grin bled away; he looked suddenly humorless. "People exceed their use," he said. "Take

Grab, for instance, he was *extremely* useful, but he also had a very big mouth. You, on the other hand, were simply in the wrong place at the wrong time, and there's just a chance that you know too much. Sorry."

"Hold on a minute! Wrong place? What place? I don't know anything about anything. Are you crazy?"

"No. I'm Mixer. Good-bye, young fool."

The gnome straightened his crossbow, but just as he was about to fire, something dropped on him. The barrowbird, which had followed the duo religiously from the Ferret and possessed the kind of frenzied death dive that others of the avian family could only dream of, subsequently exploded in a flapping, squawking cacophony.

During the struggle, Jimmy heard a click and a snap, and then he flew backward. Fast.

There was a heavy, sonorous clunk as he hit the giant bell.

Then he fell.

Down.

Dowwnn.

Dowwwnnn . . .

Mixer finally managed to shake off the bird and

swiftly realign his crossbow to bring it down with a bolt. He missed.

The barrowbird soared back into the sky and flew away.

TWENTY-SIX

THE YOWLER KNOWN as Lopsalm was an undiluted lunatic. At least, he was acting like an undiluted lunatic, and Obegarde suspected that the man might be a very good actor. He certainly had the "crazed priest" archetype down to a tee.

Lopsalm was perched atop a communion table in the southern wing of the church, his hands tied behind his back in some sort of supplication ritual, and his small, bearded face enclosed in one of the weirdest cowls Obegarde had ever laid eyes on. The cloth monstrosity, apart from its giant hood, had six wayward cords that hung down to cover the priest's ears, and almost extended past his scrawny neck as well.

"Don't you speak to me like that!" he snapped at the investigator. "How dare you come in here and fire your ignorant questions at me. I, who am of the Chalice."

"I'm sorry," said Obegarde. "I didn't think 'You must be Lopsalm?' was a particularly intrusive question."

"Hah! That's what they all say!"

"Listen—"

"What? Where?"

Obegarde rolled his eyes. "No, listen to me. I need to ask you a few more intrusive questions. If it helps any, I'll break your neck unless I'm completely satisfied."

"It's like that, is it?"

"It is."

Lopsalm scratched his wiry beard. "Go on, then, if you must!"

Obegarde slid an old cloth robe off the table and took a seat beside the priest, who immediately spun around to face him.

"Do you know any gnomes who might work here?"

"Yes and no."

"Meaning?"

"Well, he comes here. But I've never seen him do any work."

Obegarde smiled. "What's his name?"

"Tricky."

"He's called Tricky the gnome?"

"No, he isn't. I meant it's tricky to remember what his name is. Mixer, I believe, or perhaps Twixer; something of that variety. I've only met him once, and I wasn't too impressed. He's supposed to guard the sacred books."

"I see. And he doesn't do his job properly?"

"He read more than he guarded. Obsessed with them, he was. He was only here three days when the big book went missing. Haven't seen him since. Less astute minds might consider that a coincidence."

"But not you," said Obegarde with a grin. "You obviously think he stole it."

"Not at all. I reckon he was given it."

"By who?"

Lopsalm shrugged. "The Lark was fairly fond of him; she spent a lot of time teaching him the ways of Doiley."

"Doiley?"

"God of Stone; Lord Immortal and creator of the original rock."

Obegarde frowned. "The original rock? What's that?"

"Ha! Ignoramus! It's *the* rock, the rock upon
which the foundations of Illmoor were set. The living rock, the rock immortal. The rock that is none
other than the Great Yowler himself, deep in his
thousand-year slumber."

"Oh, come on. Living rock? You don't honestly
believe all that rubbish?"

"It's written in the sacred book; of course I
believe it. The sacred book tells no lies. It forecasts
a time when the Great Yowler will rise. They tell of
the second coming of Doiley, the prophet who'll
bring about his resurrection."

"Second coming? What happened the first
time?"

"He didn't quite manage it."

"Oh, right. I'm sorry to hear that."

"As are we all. Nevertheless, he will come again.
Our Lady Lauris assures us that it is so."

"Lady—"

"Lauris. We call her the Lark."

"Ah, yes, I remember you mentioning her. She
runs the church?"

"No one runs it. We're an autonomous collective; all are equal in the eyes of Yowler. We, that is,
myself, the Lark, the behemoth called Moors, and

his spindly friend Edwy, are all even-footed. However, the Lark has . . . strong beliefs."

"Stronger than yours?"

"Stronger than most."

"And why would this Lark give your gnome the sacred book? More to the point, if you're all equals, why did you let her?"

Lopsalm fiddled with the strange cloth hat. "I've told you too much already," he said without feeling.

"Oh, I don't doubt you've told me everything, yet you've shown me nothing. Clever."

"Clever? Ha! I've betrayed church secrets, and I've double-crossed friends! I've endangered my standing in the high order; I've put my soul at risk! Indeed, my only consolation will be that you won't live to tell anyone about my indiscretion."

"Ah, that explains the smile," Obegarde said. "You're planning to have me killed."

"Oh, no, Mr. Obegarde. You planned to have yourself killed the moment you stuck your nose where it wasn't wanted."

The investigator peered around. "There's nobody here," he said. "I could just kill you now. . . ."

"You could, but I don't think you will. After all, if you did strike me down, the rest of my order would make it their business to have you sent straight back to Dorley House. . . ."

Obegarde froze. "What?"

"Dorley House, in Spittle? Isn't that the breeding ground where most of your pathetic kind struggle to exist? Isn't that the wretched pit where all the poor, breadline loftwings are forced into servitude? And isn't that why you came to the city, to make enough money so that you might forget your terrible origins?"

The investigator's expression hadn't changed.

"We are Yowlers, Mr. Obegarde," Lopsalm continued. "We have the dirt on everyone and every*thing* in Illmoor. How else do you think we hold sway? In fact, I believe you have an appointment at the palace tonight?"

"How—"

"Let's see if you can survive the night to keep it."

Obegarde turned very slowly and headed for the nearest door. Halfway across the sanctuary, he stopped and looked back at Lopsalm's evil grin. "This isn't over," he said.

"Oh, it is, Mr. Obegarde. I assure you it is."

Obegarde departed the sanctuary and didn't look back until he realized that he'd taken the wrong door. Still suffering from the shock of Lopsalm's revealed knowledge, he stumbled upon a strangled route through a twisted maze of passageways into the southern wing of the church.

He walked on, and was nearing a possible exit, when he spied a thickset ogre standing sentry under three small alcoves. Two of the alcoves, one on either side, contained heavy volumes with elaborate hand-embroidered covers. The middle one was empty.

Obegarde narrowed his eyes, trying to force himself to think clearly.

A dark religion, a sacred book gone, a gnome assassin on the loose, and a giant machine camou-flaged in a dockyard warehouse. There was some kind of connection there, something he just couldn't put his finger on—

CRASH!

Obegarde looked up as a giant skylight of red and purple stained glass imploded, spewing a rain of needle-sharp shards and a man with an arrow pro-truding from his shoulder. The latter landed heavily on the thick pile of altar carpet, then rolled onto his back and lay there like a fallen angel. He didn't move.

The ogre sentry had moved with remarkable speed for a creature of its size and, having grabbed a spear from a concealed alcove, was currently edging toward the wounded stranger with a demonic but careful expression on its face.

Luckily, Obegarde reached the man first. He crouched down beside him, checked for a pulse, and then wasted no time in yanking the bolt from Jimmy's shoulder.

"*Aaahhhhhhh!!*"

The ogre leaped back, taking up a defensive position in front of the two display cases. It was soon joined by Lopsalm, who hurried in from the main sanctuary, screaming blasphemy on all enemies of the church.

"*Ahhhhhhh!! Myshoullderrdamnitt!*" Jimmy cried. He reached up a hand to cover his wound, but Obegarde already had a palm pressed hard against it. The thief felt an alien heat surging through him, strengthening his bones and doubling his resistance to the agony in his shoulder. It lasted no more than a few seconds, and then it was gone. So was the pain.

Jimmy sat up, befuddled and half conscious.

"Th-thanks," he said. "Saved me, saved Jimmy. For a bet. Roof. Fell. Gnome. Had a crossbow. Death, dead Jimmy. I'm alive. Is it? Who said that? Where am I, then? Bye."

He slumped back. Obegarde leaned over him to ensure that the wound had healed, but a second crossbow bolt thudded into the carpet beside them. Unlike the bolt he'd pulled from the stranger, this one was silver-edged. Obegarde glanced up through the serrated hole in the window and saw the gnome with brass teeth glaring down at him.

Just as a third bolt flew from its housing, Obegarde backflipped and sprang to his feet. Then, dragging Jimmy's semiconscious form into the shadows, he bolted from the hall, shoving Lopsalm aside and dodging a (thankfully) badly aimed spear thrown by the ogre sentry.

"Get after him!" Lopsalm screamed, shaking his fists at the distant head of the gnome. "He'll ruin everything! Well?" He spun around and jabbed an accusatory finger at the ogre. "What do you think you're doing?"

"Lookin' fo' me spear, guv'nor."

"Well, don't! You see that ragtag scruffian over there? I want you to pick him up an' wring his damn neck!"

"How does I do that, then, guv'nor?"

"I don't know! You're the bloody ogre; you figure it out!"

TWENTY-SEVEN

IT WAS EVENING in Dullitch, and the peaceful sleep of the three or four decent citizens still residing in the city was being disturbed by the unmistakable sound of crossbow fire.

In the extreme northeast of the church district, two figures sped along the rooftops, leaping gantries and skirting chimney pots as if they were mere markers on a predestined course. You could tell it was a death chase. The big man in front took no measure of his jumps, invariably landing a few inches short of every adjoining rooftop he made for, and ending up scrabbling for purchase on the lower slates. Also, the way the pursuer hurried around the weather vanes with his crossbow instead of lifting the weapon strategically over them, indicated that he was a gnome; a gnome with a grudge (and a crossbow, obviously).

As he ran, Obegarde reflected on his quality of life.

Most of all, he hated the rooftop chases.

Dressed in a flowing coat, which seemed as much a peril of the chase as the gnome behind him, he came to an abrupt halt on the summit of the Treasury. Putting a hand to his rib cage, he groaned as his bruises bit him: he hadn't the time to heal. Then, breath freezing on the air, he peered over his shoulder to see whether Mixer had given up. A small explosion just left of his earlobe suggested that, on the contrary, the little bastard was quite prepared to make a night of it. The thought persisting, Obegarde took to his feet again. The gnome followed.

On the narrow ledge atop the Diamond Clock Tower, a slate slid away and smashed onto the cobbles far below. Obegarde made the decision to ignore it a little too late, and crashed onto the dark, shadowy roof of the History Museum. The impact wasn't flattering; a thousand heroes had made the drop with a lot more style and a lot less fuss, but Obegarde wasn't a hero. He was just a man falling onto a museum roof. There was a difference.

The sky over Dullitch was moving fast; it had

already gathered an army of clouds in preparation for the downtime drizzle. Obegarde scrambled for purchase on a bell's housing as another bolt exploded three inches from his right elbow. Suddenly, looking back across the midnight cityscape, he realized there was nowhere to run. The rooftop of the Steeplejack Inn was too far away, and in order to reach Tyrell Tower he'd have to go back past the Diamond Clock. It was all over, then, no question. He closed his eyes and tried to think of a god who might be merciful. None sprang to mind, but then Obegarde wasn't exactly the most religious man in the city; he'd only visited the church once in two years, and that had been to retrieve a stolen crate of Bhorkan Red from the vestry. Shaking himself from his reverie, he tried to review his options. He had about five or six seconds, tops.

Thwack! Another bolt was released in the darkness behind him.

Eyes tightly shut, jaw hardened, Obegarde turned and waited for the agonizing impact of the bolt.

Thunk. The bolt ricocheted from the roof beside him, split the slates in two, and dismissed another cracked shard to the cobbles below.

Obegarde swallowed and thanked his stars; as luck would have it, Mixer was aiming badly.

Thwack! A new bolt flew away on the wind.

Obegarde sprang up, eyes darting from side to side as he searched for an easy exit.

Thunk. An arrow this time; the little demon must have changed ammunition. The head bit into Obegarde's chest and he tumbled from the church roof. For a few fleeting seconds, the air whistled in his ears. Then he hit the grass. Hard.

Groaning with the pain of the fall, Obegarde reached a hand to his chest, removed the arrow and tossed it aside. Then he closed his eyes and tried to heal.

Loftwings possess many little idiosyncrasies that separate them from the pure breed. These include the laying on of hands, a swift recovery from all non-anointed wounds and, if concentration allows, a remarkable ability to play dead.

Silence reigned in the cemetery.

At length, footsteps neared, and Mixer loomed into view.

The gnome, crossbow still clenched tightly in his hands, put a foot to the investigator's chest and gave him an experimental nudge. When he got no response, he dropped the weapon, put a hand inside his jerkin, and drew out a fistful of red powder. Countless grains poured from between his fingers.

Mixer cast the powder to the floor beside the investigator and mumbled something unintelligible under his breath. There was a sudden eruption of white flame. It was accompanied by a low, resounding hum.

Obegarde allowed his eyelids to part a fraction.

What's this now? he thought. Don't tell me the little freak's a wizard as well as a murdering thug?

The flame died away. In its place stood a woman of striking appearance. She was raven-haired and wearing far fewer clothes than respectability demanded. An air of dark magic surrounded her. She looked down at Mixer's wretched face with something approaching disgust.

"What now?" she demanded.

"It's me, Mixer," the gnome began. "I have news."

"Well?"

"It's the loftwing I was telling you about, mistress—"

"Ha! That was days ago. You've only just managed to catch up with him? Insufferable! I'm sure I don't know why Lopsalm hired you; that wretched creature might have told the palace *anything* in the time it's taken you to silence him."

"Yes, mistress, but I've done it now. My work is over, and all our enemies have been subdued. The thief is a memory, and Master Lopsalm is dealing with his young friend."

The Lark raised an eyebrow expectantly. "Good," she said slowly. "But there is still much to do. You have the book?"

"Yes," Mixer went on, his eyes glazed with uncertainty. "Shouldn't we tell Master Lopsalm about it?"

"Lopsalm already knows."

"But, mistress, you said it was *our* secret."

"Yes, well . . . just make sure the book is safe." The Lark smiled. "As for you, Mixer, I'm still a little confused as to how this 'investigator' chanced upon you in the first place."

"I've been thinking about that, mistress," Mixer intoned, choosing his words carefully. "Perhaps someone at the palace suspected yo—"

"Me? You dare to suggest that I am the weak link?"

"No, no, of course not, mistress. Is it not possible that we might have a spy in our midst?"

"A spy?"

"Yes, mistress. Are you sure the others are reliable?"

The Lark nodded. "Absolutely," she said. "The followers share a common purpose. Besides, Moors and Edwy don't have the imagination required for betrayal."

"No, mistress. I'll, er, I'll bring the book to you, then."

"No! Just hide it. The city *must not* find out what we're up to. They still have time to ruin everything we've worked so hard to achieve! So keep that book safe. Also, have the receptacle moved."

"Wh-what, mistress? The machine? But it's huge! Where else can—"

"I don't care, but you must let me know *where* it ends up so that I may aim the ray correctly. Somewhere in the center of the city would be preferable. A rooftop; I'm assuming you still have the Dust of Levitation?"

"Yes, mistress."

"Very good; it took a great deal of bartering to obtain. Communicate with me again when the task is done. Our whole religion is counting on you."

"Wait, mistress!"

The image shimmered, but did not disappear. "Well?"

Mixer shifted uncomfortably. "What of Moors and Edwy, mistress? Did they get the lizards to Plunge without incident?"

"Indeed. They are testing the remarkable properties of our scaly little friends right at this moment. Very successfully, I might add. The villagers of Plunge are simply . . . lost for words. Glory awaits."

Mixer nodded. "We're almost ready, then!" he hazarded.

"Almost," the Lark confirmed. "When the lighthouse lens intensifies our glare, we will be able to fire upon Dullitch. The city will be no more, and our select brotherhood will reign. Just remember to leave *after* you've moved the machine. If it is discovered, all our hard work will have been in vain."

A nod; Mixer bowed low.

"I'll not fail you, mistress," he said. "And then, maybe I can join you in Plunge?"

The image in the flame said nothing more; it merely flickered and melted away. Mixer took a moment to stop shaking, then crouched down to retrieve his crossbow. His fingers had just found the handle, when Obegarde sprang to his feet and stamped on them.

TWENTY-EIGHT

BACK IN THE CHURCH, things were not going well for Jimmy Quickstint. . . .

The ogre had snatched him up by a thatch of hair, spun him around, and fastened him in a head-lock.

Jimmy kicked out with both arms and legs, flailing wildly against the stranglehold, which the ogre promptly began to close like a vise.

Using a technique familiar to many stalwart wrigglers of the thieving trade, Jimmy allowed himself to go limp and then, when the grip loosened, attempted to slide between the legs of his aggressor and sweep the beast off its feet with a well-aimed tendon kick.

It didn't work.

The ogre, whose legs were as thick as tree trunks,

simply scooped Jimmy up again, snapping him back into the headlock with comparative ease.

However, this time Jimmy was closer to the wall. Releasing a reserve of strength he hadn't previously been aware of, he leaped up with both feet and, placing them flat against the stone, launched himself and the ogre backward. They flew into the nearest display case, which shattered and collapsed under the ogre's weight.

Jimmy was first to his feet. Snatching up a sacred Shindu cannonball, he swung around with both arms and struck the ogre a glancing blow across the back of its skull. The beast gave a dull grunt and slumped forward.

Jimmy dropped the cannonball and fell against the rough stone of the chamber wall, his breath coming in slow gasps. He closed his eyes.

As weeks go, he thought, I've had better. I've been conned by a one-armed thief, pursued by a blasphemous bird, shot at by a gnome with brass teeth, healed by some stranger in a dirty coat, and strangled by a bloody great ogre. And it's only Tuesday.

Jimmy took a deep breath. When he opened his eyes again, Lopsalm was right beside him. The priest was displaying a nice warm smile, and a dagger.

"That was a very lucky escape," he said. "But now it is time for you to die."

Jimmy's punch caught the mad priest completely by surprise and practically knocked him into next week. He followed it up with a second—slightly weaker—but still on target. Lopsalm staggered sideways and dropped his weapon. Then he turned and fled from the chamber.

"Get after him!" came a familiar squawk.

Jimmy looked up at the barrowbird. "What?"

"Get after the priest!"

"No way!" he screamed. "That's the first person who's ever run away from me; I'm not gonna push my luck."

"If you lose him," the bird snapped, "I'll plague you forever. Now get going!"

"Why can't you follow him?"

"I'm gonna see if I can find the gnome and that other bloke. I'll catch up with you afterward."

"Promise?"

"Yes! Now move!"

Jimmy mustered all his strength and bolted from the church. When he arrived outside, the street was dark. He glanced left and right, trying to distinguish any shape that might be moving faster than those around it. Just as he was about to shrug the whole thing off and make his way back inside, he spotted Lopsalm's floppy hat. It was lying at the mouth of Westcoat Alley, a dim slit that formed a shortcut between Dullitch's Merchant Quarter and the City Cathedral.

Jimmy kicked the hat aside and cautiously entered the alley.

TWENTY-NINE

OBEGARDE HAD MIXER pinned to the ground.

He rested the edge of the crossbow on the gnome's throat and applied gentle pressure.

"Noooo!" Mixer moaned, eyes streaming with tears. "Pleeasse."

"Quiet," snapped Obegarde. "Now, I'm going to talk and you're going to listen very carefully. Nod if you understand."

Mixer made a slight inclination with his head, but the bolt dug into his throat and drew a thick line of blood.

"Okay," the investigator continued. "The Lark and her people aren't your friends. They saw you taking an interest in the scriptures and they've brainwashed you."

Mixer struggled, but Obegarde increased pressure on the bolt and almost choked the gnome into unconsciousness.

"They've had you running around for them," he continued, "doing all the dangerous work; things *you* could be hung for. Whereas they, they haven't done anything illegal, at least nothing provable. Now do you understand what I'm saying?"

The gnome ceased his struggles and appeared, just for a second, to be paying attention.

"You're lying," he managed, his lips moist with spittle. "They need me; I'm a vital part of the group. The Mistress and Master Lopsalm will rule, and I'll be at their right hand!"

"Ah. That's why they've left you here, is it?" said Obegarde. "Here in Dullitch, where everything's going to be turned to stone. From what I heard, those other two cultist clowns are away on the wind and, as for Lopsalm, I'll bet he's already killed that poor lad and spirited himself off to Plunge! Don't look at me like that; you know I'm right. From what I hear, this group of yours is stabbing one another in the back and using you to do it!"

Mixer shook his head, and Obegarde could see that all the terrible consequences of the gnome's actions were dawning on him at once. As Obegarde released his viselike grip on the crossbow, the gnome brought his hands to his face and wept.

"I wanted to be an assassin," he sniffed. "But I failed the initiation so they banished me to the church as a cleaner. A cleaner, me! Well, I showed them. Master Lopsalm, and the Lark, they gave me *purpose*. First I kept the sacred book and then, when the thief returned from Grinswood with the lizards . . ."

"Lizards?"

". . . he knew too much, so I took him down. I only scared the old man. Of course, they *wanted* me to kill him."

"That's enough, I think. You can explain all this to the viscount."

"You don't understand. I—"

"Come on," said Obegarde, dragging him up from the floor. "I'll take you to jail. The Crown can decide your fate in the morning." He straightened up, shouldered the crossbow, and pushed the gnome in front of him. "And if you try anything smart, you'll find out why the world hates a loftwing."

Mixer coughed and managed half a nod.

"Good. Now, keep your hands where I can see them."

He shoved the gnome in the back with his boot, and the two of them headed on down the hill.

High in the sky, the barrowbird watched them with considerable interest.

THIRTY

T HE ALLEY was wreathed in shadow.

Jimmy Quickstint picked his way, catlike, between crumpled bins and bulging rubbish sacks that spilled their contents from gaping wounds. Occasionally he would stand stock-still and listen for the slightest hint of movement ahead. Then, detecting nothing, he would move on much as before, hands bunched into fists for the attack he expected at any moment.

Then he saw Lopsalm. The mad priest was a tiny speck at the farthest end of the alley, about to cross Cathedral Street.

Slowly at first, then picking up speed, Jimmy moved faster and faster until he was hurtling head-long after the priest, arms pumping and legs threatening to strike every inch of the way.

What am I doing now? he thought. Eleven o'clock at night and, when I should be tucked up in bed, I'm chasing a religious lunatic down a blind alley at the request of a bloody pigeon. I must be mad; there's no other explanation. Never mind, I've nearly caught him. Oh look, he's going in to the cathedral grounds. I wonder if Jed's working tonight?

THIRTY-ONE

THE LOFTWING BRANCH of the vampire family was characterized by its breathtaking reflexes, which were described by some anthropologists as "so fast as to be almost anticipatory." Mixer, on the other hand, was desperate, and occasionally desperation carries an amazing ability to turn back the odds.

They were approaching Dullitch City Jail when the gnome made his move. Obegarde, who'd had the nose of the crossbow jammed into Mixer's back since the moment he'd hoisted him off the cobbles, was beginning to relax. The jail loomed into view at the end of the street, and manholes aside, there was simply nowhere for the little gnome to go.

Then, without the slightest physical indication, Mixer took off like a torpedo . . . *toward* the jailhouse. Wary and not a little baffled, Obegarde rocketed after him, slowing a bit when he realized the gnome was on a collision course with the jail's immense barred door. But Mixer knew exactly what he was doing.

"Hey, stop him!" Obegarde screamed at the sentries when he saw the little gnome squeeze himself between the bars and disappear into the darkness beyond.

The two guards on duty began to stumble about in confusion, partly befuddled and partly bemused at the fact that someone had just forced their way *into* the building. Mixer evaded them with consummate ease, sliding between their clumsy limbs and leading them on a merry dance along the gloomy corridors of the jail.

Obegarde arrived at the entrance to the jailhouse, crashing into the giant door and hammering on the bars until his knuckles bled.

"Let me in, you fools! He's going to get away!"

"Leave this to us, citizen!" the guards bellowed back. "We have everything under control."

"Like hell you do! LET ME IN!"

There was a lengthy pause, and the gate began to trundle sideways. Obegarde grabbed at the retreating bar and propelled himself inside.

Unfortunately, he then ran smack-bang into the one person in Dullitch he always tried passionately to avoid: Quartermaster Alan Sorrow.

"Obegarde, what a lovely surprise; and where do you think *you're* going?"

Sorrow wasn't a well-liked man in Dullitch. In fact, he was positively loathed. This was something he simply couldn't fathom, for, being one of the four quartermasters, he considered himself highly respectable. Obegarde, on the other hand, he regarded as a hopeless piece of street scum. This didn't worry the loftwing unduly, as the feeling was mutual.

"Alan," he said breathlessly, "you've got to let me pass. There's a gnome on the loose in there."

"Yes, it seems so," Sorrow agreed, nodding his head to one side and listening as a hundred pairs of feet responded to the unmistakable din of the jailhouse alarm. "Do you have any idea why that is?"

"Yes," the loftwing managed. "I brought him in. Now, can I—"

"Hold your horses, Obegarde. My men will handle it. What's the charge?"

"Um . . . murder, assault, possible theft, conspiracy to endanger the city, er, you name it. . . ."

"I see. Nice of you to let him go, then."

"What? I *didn't* let him go."

"Then, would you like to explain what he's doing running loose around my jailhouse?"

"He escaped."

"Terrific. Well, we'll handle it from here. We are, after all, *professionals*."

Obegarde snorted. "You're a bunch of incompetents," he muttered.

"What was that?"

"I said, you're a bun—"

"Yes, I heard you the first time; I just wanted to see if a bloodsucker like yourself had the nerve to repeat it. I have to confess, I'm shocked." He stepped forward, ushering Obegarde into the street, and motioned for the great gates to be closed behind him.

"You're coming with me," he said flatly.

"Where?"

"The palace. I understand Lord Curfew's secretary wants to see you, though I can't think why the palace would employ a *freelancer* when they've got us."

THIRTY-TWO

THE ANCIENT GATES barring entrance to the grounds of Dullitch Cathedral creaked ominously in the wind; the chains that usually constricted them had been severed.

"Watch your back here, boy," said the barrow-bird, landing on the iron gatepost. "I reckon that Lopsalm could be a tricky customer."

"Thanks," said Jimmy wretchedly. "I'll keep that in mind when he's beating my brains out with a candlestick."

"No need for sarcasm; I'm just trying to help."

"Thanks." Jimmy spotted a shadow slipping between two stone monuments and crouched down to hide himself in the long-neglected grass. A few seconds later the shadow emerged and, looking both ways, nipped behind another statue. It was definitely Lopsalm; the little priest's pathetically scrawny form gave him away.

"Out of his bloody mind," muttered the barrowbird. "That's one of the requirements of being a priest, if you ask me. Start a bloke off wearing a dress and sooner or later things are bound to go wrong."

"You may have stumbled upon something there," said Jimmy.

"What's that?"

"Well, wizards wear robes and most of them go bad. There was one up in, there was one, er, I don't remember. . . ." Jimmy trailed off. He knew that he must be pretty scared, subconsciously, because he'd started talking for the sake of talking, and that was always a sure sign of trouble.

He kept himself low to the ground and pulled himself along on his stomach. The damp from the grass seeped into his clothes and, somewhere behind him in the darkness, a flapping indicated that the barrowbird had moved skyward to get a better view of the proceedings.

Lopsalm was clearly visible now, and his destination was equally obvious. The scabby little priest was heading for the hulking mass of the cathedral. He broke into a run and had almost cleared the first flight of steps when he tripped and fell.

The barrowbird flapped furiously. "Now! Quick, while the bugger's down!"

Jimmy bolted. Running faster than he'd ever run before, he cleared bushes and gravestones with jumps that would've ruined a shorter man for life. Lopsalm was getting to his feet when the gravedigger cannonballed into him. The two men rolled on the ground, raining blows on each other in the familiar fashion of men who've never fought before and are trying to remember how their fathers had told them to bunch a fist.

Jimmy scored the first "oof," but spent too long congratulating himself and got caught across the chin with a brass knuckle-duster Lopsalm had seemingly produced from thin air.

"The Holy Hand of Yowl!" yelled the priest, his grin ethereal in the moonlight. "How it striketh thee down!"

Jimmy brought up a knee and, more from luck than judgment, connected with the man's most sacred relics.

"The, er, Gravedigger's Thrust of Doom," he barked back. "How it maketh your eyes water!"

Lopsalm creased up and collapsed, something that Jimmy mistakenly interpreted as license for a breather. He struggled to his feet, took a step back, and tripped over the edge of a gravestone. When he managed to struggle up again, the priest had vanished.

"You silly bugger!" squawked the barrowbird, flapping on the wind. "You shouldn't have taken your eyes off him!"

Jimmy groaned. "Did you see where he went?"

"Yeah; in there."

The cathedral loomed large. Jimmy hoped it didn't look as bad on the inside, but something about the expressions of the gargoyles suggested the architect had been working on a theme of unimaginable terror.

"Well, here goes nothing," he said, and sprinted off, the barrowbird close behind him.

THIRTY-THREE

AN EAR-SPLITTING scream echoed through the palace corridors. There was a lengthy pause, then . . .

"What is the meaning of this disruption?" the viscount boomed. He'd been somewhat taken aback when Secretary Spires had rushed into his private chambers (once again without knocking) accompanied by a bedraggled stranger in a dirty overcoat. He made a mental note to execute his chamber guards, assuming he could find them.

Obegarde, still panting heavily from the night's exertions, took a step back and collapsed into one of the palace's hard marble chairs. Spires was less keen to be silent, and stood at the edge of Curfew's desk, his hands visibly shaking.

"Now," the viscount began, "I'm sure you're

here on the most urgent of business, but still, I'd appreciate it if you at least made an attempt to announce yourself. These intrusions really are most . . ." He trailed off as he saw the secretary's expression. "What is it, man?"

"I have vital news, Excellency."

"What news? Who is *this* fellow?"

"First things first, master. The young lady you asked me to trace—I searched the palace for info, asked every employee. I turned up nothing."

"Unfortunate . . ."

"Yes, but then I spoke to the Yowlers."

"You did what? Without my permission! You imbecile! You do realize that anything you say reflects on me? Do you know how many Yowler groups there are in this city? Moreover, do you know how many Yowlers there are in *this quarter* of the city? If you've compromised my posit—"

"Don't worry, Excellency! Please, don't worry! The news isn't as bad as we think—"

"Oh, it's bad all right," Obegarde interrupted.

"Quiet! You'll get your turn, whoever you are."

"I'm just saying—"

"Well, don't. Let him finish. Go on, Spires."

The secretary passed a set of parchments to the

viscount. "I think you should take a look at these profiles, Excellency."

Curfew studied the scrolls, his cheek twitching as his eyes progressed down each page.

"Moors, Edwy, the Lark? Who *are* these people?"

"A breakaway section of the Yowlers, Excellency."

"How breakaway, exactly? Breakaway as in still tied to, or breakaway as in totally broken? I don't want to end up murdered in my bed—"

"They're total outcasts, Excellency; I assure you. They deserted the main order last year to start up on their own. The ruling brotherhood say they won't have anything to do with them because they're all mad."

Curfew swallowed a few times and wiped his brow with the back of his hand.

Spires slowly took back the parchments and continued. "Moors, Edwy, and Lopsalm are all ex-priests from the order. We think the fourth member, the one known as the Lark, might be our girl Lauris."

Curfew snatched the parchments back and rifled through them. "Hmm . . . these aren't very good. Apart from the fact that this *Moors* is supposed to be grossly obese, we don't have an awful lot to go on; most of these pictures are drawn in crayon."

"Yes, Excellency—our artist *was* working from a few vague descriptions. But wait! There's more. The Yowlers say that one of their grand churches was recently sold to this Lopsalm character for a sum referred to as considerable."

"Let me guess: Karuim's?"

"Precisely, Excellency. Used to be the temple of origins, didn't it?"

Curfew perked up. "But that's next door, for goodness' sake! We can storm it."

"Unfortunately not, Excellency. The church is on Yowler land, and even though they're opposed to the new order, we'll incur their considerable wrath if we thunder right in there with no religious jurisdiction."

"Absolutely, absolutely. We don't want that kind of trouble. . . . You'll have to think of something else. Where does this fellow come in?"

The loftwing stepped forward and gave a reluctant bow.

"This is Mr. Obegarde, Excellency, the investigator we hired to track Lauris."

Curfew nodded. "Ah yes, last I heard you were

chasing after a gnome who worked as a cleaner at the church?"

"Oh, he's a cleaner all right," Obegarde conceded. "He's also an assassin, a thief, a conspirator, and only the gods know what else."

"Definitely a member of the group, then?"

"Oh yes."

"Did you catch him?"

"I did, and I took him to the city jail."

"He's there now?"

"I doubt it."

"Oh?"

"He got away from me in the jailhouse. Sorrow's men might catch him, but I wouldn't build your hopes up. . . ."

The viscount caressed his eyelids with a thumb and a forefinger.

"I see," he said sadly. "And do we have any idea, absolutely *any* idea, what all this is about?"

"Not really," Obegarde admitted. "All I've got is a few fractured facts from eavesdropping and a very dodgy confession from our little friend. What I *do* know is this: there's a machine in a warehouse down at the harbor; it's big, it's mean, and it's definitely a vital part of whatever this group has planned. If we can do a demolition job on the cursed thing, my bet is we'd be putting a major dent in their plans. It's in Warehouse Six."

Curfew nodded. "Spires," he began, gripping the arms of his chair so hard that his fingernails turned white, "I want you to take all available guards and destroy this machine. Do it quickly. Do it now. I'll come along for good measure. Anything else that might help?"

"Possibly," Obegarde said when Spires had hurried from the room. "The Lark has gone to Plunge."

"Plunge? But that's miles away. Have you any idea why?"

"No, but she had a thief steal some lizards from a forest up north, and then the gnome killed him. Now her minions have them; as far as I can make out, they're en route to rendezvous with her."

"In Plunge?"

"Yes. Whatever she's planning, I'm guessing these lizards are an integral part of it."

At that moment, Spires returned. He stood in the corridor, fully armored and gasping for air.

"The men are ready, Excellency," he said.

THIRTY-FOUR

HAVING SHINNED UP a sheer brick wall in the nave of the cathedral, Jimmy Quickstint vaulted over the edge of a balcony and landed, on all fours, in the dark antechamber beyond.

"Bugger this," he spat at the barrowbird who flew over the balcony to land beside him. "He could be anywhere."

"Just stay alert, boy. I'll keep watch for you."

Jimmy squinted into the gloomy shadows cast by the cathedral's innards. He nipped over to crouch beside a heavy iron pipe that ran from floor to ceiling, and put an ear to the outer shell.

"What're you doing, boy?"

"Shhh! It's an old thief trick."

"You were a thief?"

"Be quiet!"

Jimmy strained to listen; somewhere far off in the gargantuan sanctuary, he heard the unmistakable click of a door closing.

"Well," squawked the barrowbird. "Getting anything?"

"Mmm . . . I think he's downstairs."

"Straight up? How can you tell?"

Jimmy tapped the pipe indicatively and raised an eyebrow. "A door closed."

"Ah. How do you know it was him, though?" asked the barrowbird. "There must be folk working here, place this size: bishops, canon, cardinals, and the like."

"Cathedral's abandoned," Jimmy snapped. "Didn't you see the chain on the gates? No one comes here now, not since the Yowlers outlawed other religions. The grounds 're still used for burials, but that's about it."

The catacombs beneath Dullitch Cathedral were legendary.

Stretching for half a mile in every direction, they linked up with the city's equally legendary sewer system. Rumor suggested that black elves wandered the subterranean waterways, but no one had survived long enough to prove it.

Jimmy, with the barrowbird perched jauntily on his shoulder, squinted ahead. The passageway he'd happened upon culminated in a T-junction, and the figure lingering there was definitely not a black elf. Jimmy couldn't be sure, but he hoped it was the rogue Yowler priest.

"Hey, you! Stop in the name of, er—"

"Jort," said the barrowbird.

"Yes! Stop in the name of Jort!"

The figure at the end of the tunnel paused, shook a fist in Jimmy's direction, and disappeared left.

"Who's Jort?" said the gravedigger, hurrying after him.

"Powerful god."

"Really? I've never heard of him."

"No, well, I can't say I'm totally shocked. He doesn't get much publicity in these parts."

Jimmy nodded. "Who does?"

They pursued Lopsalm to the end of the tunnel, where a door gaped open to reveal an ancient and precipitously steep staircase. Footsteps were just barely audible some six or seven flights up.

"Where d'you reckon they go?" asked the barrowbird.

Jimmy shrugged. "A fair way, I imagine. Judging from the echo, they might even lead to the cathedral roof."

"Incredible! The architect who built this place must've been out of his bloody mind."

"Or religious," Jimmy added. "In practice, it seems to amount to the same thing."

The stairs went on and on. Jimmy counted more than four hundred before they ran out on him. There was an old wooden trapdoor in the ceiling, and nowhere else to go.

He took a second to sniff the air and cautiously lifted the door. A blanket of rain splattered on his face.

Thunder rumbled overhead.

The barrowbird took off.

Jimmy padded out onto the flat expanse of the roof. Unfortunately, before Jimmy could begin the hunt, Lopsalm dropped from a gargoyle's outstretched wing and clubbed him on the back of the neck with a candlestick.

Lopsalm stepped forward, his lips curled in a terrible smile.

He reached down and snatched hold of Jimmy's

leg. Then he dragged the gravedigger into the center of the cathedral roof and, after observing his handiwork for a few minutes, produced a minibow from the depths of his robe.

"Your death will be . . . interesting," he muttered. "Certainly not fast, but enjoyable nevertheless."

Jimmy was beginning to come round, his vision clearing to reveal the demonic features of Lopsalm, and beyond, a tiny black speck descending from the sky at an alarming rate. The priest noticed Jimmy's wandering gaze.

Lopsalm stepped back and squinted up at the sky, mere seconds before the barrowbird came into view. He raised the minibow and fired. The arrow arced into the air, striking the bird with such force that it flew backward a few feet before it began to plummet.

But the bird's diversion had bought Jimmy a few valuable seconds. The gravedigger catapulted himself to his feet, kicked the bow from Lopsalm's grasp, and shoved the priest backward, hard.

Lopsalm faltered and tried to right himself, but it was too late. Jimmy lashed out with a fist and sent the Yowler priest hurtling dangerously close to the edge of the cathedral roof. Lopsalm managed to snatch at a protruding slate and save himself, but as he struggled to regain his footing, the momentum of his impromptu flight overtook him.

Jimmy saw his chance.

He leaped, landing with a well-placed boot in the middle of Lopsalm's chest.

The collision was fast and furious. Lopsalm gasped and toppled backward, flapping his arms furiously in a last-ditch attempt to save himself.

A scream erupted.

And Lopsalm fell.

For a moment, there was silence.

Jimmy Quickstint, hunkered down on all fours and bleeding at the mouth, peered out over the edge of the roof. Through a blanket of fine rain, he glimpsed something very messy spread out on the steps below. The tally of Yowler followers in Dullitch, he reflected, had just gone down by one.

Jimmy sighed, and his heart slowed. He stared down dispassionately at the corpse, before the strangled cries of the barrowbird shook him from his reverie. He struggled to attain a standing position, and made his way over the damp tiles to where the bird lay squawking weakly, the arrow still protruding from its puffy breast.

"*Awwk!*"

"Be quiet. Let me pull it out."

"It's no good, mate. I'm a goner."

"Nonsense. One sharp tug and—"

"I'm telling you, boy, it's fatal. I've had it."

"Where did you get such a negative attitude?"

"No joke. I'm—I'm—I'm—"

There was a sudden, pulse-stopping pause. Then a flash of lightning arced from the sky and struck the barrowbird. Surrounded by a shimmering wave of electric energy, it squawked, shuddered, and began to change shape.

Jimmy looked on, openmouthed, as the distortion took on the recognizable form of a small and very wiry old man. He was wearing a tattered piece of cloth stretched (rather to its limits) into a sort of diaper arrangement.

Thunder rumbled. Erratic lightning flashed again, even more brilliantly than before, and the skies darkened.

"What the bloody hell is this?" shouted Jimmy. "Who are you, some kind of metamorphic wizard?"

"No, mate," said the old man, his breath beginning to fail. "Never gone much on wizardry, myself."

"Necromancer?"

"N-no."

"Sorcerer?"

"N-n-no."

"A god then, I'm guessing."

The old man shrugged. "No, th-though I was cursed by the disciples of a particularly watchful one."

Jimmy's eyes narrowed. "So you're just a mortal man who annoyed a god?"

"Ha! Y-y-you g-got it."

"Are you going to die?"

"Y-yes, but not before you promise me something."

Jimmy's concerned expression drained away; it was replaced by an apprehensive twitch. "It doesn't involve another roof, does it? I'm actually pretty terrified of heights."

"L-L-Lopsalm's n-not alone. M-make sure you g-g-get the others. T-t-terrible doooom."

"What? How *can* I? I don't even know who the others are, damn it! These are the Yowlers we're talking about. There might be hundreds of them!"

"P-p-p-promise."

"No . . ."

"P-p-p-p-promise."

"No!"

"P-p-p-p-p-promise."

"NO!"

"P-p-p . . ."

"All right, I promise!! But I can't—"

The old man died.

"Damn you!" Jimmy screamed. "Now I've made a promise I can't bloody keep. You crafty, vindictive, decrepit old . . . corpse!"

As if in reply, the skies opened up and Jimmy was pelted with hailstones. Throwing his arms up over his head, he made a valiant turn against the rain and out over the wide, statue-covered roof. With any luck he'd be able to get to the trapdoor before the gods stoned him to death. He certainly wouldn't be taking the shortcut down.

THIRTY-FIVE

THE FRENZIED ACTIVITY of the city guard had brought most of the inhabitants of the harbor district out into the streets.

Viscount Curfew, who'd decided to personally oversee the destruction of the machine in Warehouse Six, stood at the rear of the demolition team, shouting orders and offering the occasional boon of encouragement when a particularly big chunk crashed to the ground. The team, who'd obviously been informed of the machine's imminent threat to the city, were hacking away at its various extremities like men possessed, while an ogre-led brute force (employed at the very last minute by an inspired guard sergeant) made light work of the many bits the main team couldn't handle. Giant, angled mirrors came crashing to the floor, while various tubular wooden arms containing even more reflective barriers were ripped off and soundly stamped into dust. Curfew prayed to the gods of justice that those responsible surfaced quickly.

Obegarde and Spires mingled among the growing assembly of late-night harbor workers, assuring them that there was nothing to worry about, and urging them to return to their business.

"It's a routine inspection," Spires explained to one bystander, while Obegarde, bluffing with greater success, offered another the explanation that "His lordship got a letter of complaint from the Harbor Master; we don't know who owns the thing, but it's taking up far too much room."

As was usually the case in Dullitch, the crowd ended up squabbling among themselves and generally forgot what all the fuss had been about in the first place.

Curfew sidled up to his secretary. "Well, it's done, Spires," he whispered. "We've managed to destroy the machine *and* avoid any repercussions from the Yowlers."

"You think so, milord?"

"Absolutely. They can't interfere while they're trying to disassociate themselves from this breakaway

group. All we have to do now is round up the strag-
glers and haul them in. At least, all those still at large
in Dullitch."

"Very good, Excellency."

"I want you to send a group of guards to
Karuim's Church. As soon as anyone sets foot outside that building, I want them arrested."

"Yes, Excellency."

Curfew turned back to face the demolition
squad. "The most important thing would seem to be
the machine and, thankfully, we've annihilated
that." He pointed over at the massed heap of rubble.
"Dump it on a barge and ship it out!" he screamed
at the city guards. "You've done a good job, men. A
very good job!"

As the crowd dispersed, Obegarde spotted Alan
Sorrow and managed to catch up with the quartermaster before his guards vacated the warehouse.

"Yes, what is it now?"

"Did you catch the gnome?"

"Now, listen—"

Obegarde made a frantic grab for the quartermaster. "Did you or didn't you?" he yelled, as three
of Sorrow's subordinates wrenched him away from
their commander.

"No, we didn't," Sorrow fumed, shoving Obegarde into the impromptu wall formed by his men. "In fact, I very much doubt if there even *was* a frigging gno—Lord Curfew, what can we do for your excellency?"

The guard group parted to admit the viscount, Spires waddling along after him like an affectionate puppy.

"Is there a problem, here?" the viscount said.

"No problem, lordship, but this fellow here is getting to be a—"

"Hero?"

"Well, no—"

"City defender? Champion of the people? Choose your words wisely, Master Sorrow. You have the gnome known as Mixer in custody?"

Sorrow looked to his men for support but, unsurprisingly, they had all mooched away.

"Um . . . not exactly, lordship."

"I assume you're working on it."

"Absolutely, lordship."

Obegarde shook his head and marched from the warehouse. "As I said before, I wouldn't hold my breath."

THIRTY-SIX

OBEGARDE was quite surprised when, returning from the harbor district, he ran straight into the ragbag youth from the church. He was even more surprised when the stranger saw *him*, turned on his heel, and fled off up the lane.

"Hey, you! Wait there!"

The loftwing gave chase, hurtling over the cobbles and leaping the odd rubbish bin strategically kicked in his path. Eventually he cornered the stranger in an alley between Winding Way and Birch Street.

"My name's Jimmy Quickstint," Jimmy bleated. "I'm just a gravedigger. I'm not a thief, or an assassin, or a priest, or a curate, or anything to do with Yowler. I don't know how I got involved in all this— just leave me alone!"

Obegarde grinned and nodded. "Jareth Obegarde, investigator; and you're not going anywhere until you tell me why the gnome tried to kill you."

"I don't know why!" said Jimmy, exasperated. "He just *did*. He killed Grab, too."

"Grab?"

"Yeah, Grab Dafisful; mind you, that was probably due to stealin' for those cultists. That was why the bird was after him in the first place."

"What's this? A bird? I think you'd better tell me everything from the beginning."

Jimmy collapsed into a sniveling heap on the floor. "I was afraid you'd say that," he said. "But I'm tired. I'm so tired I can barely stand up."

Obegarde helped the gravedigger to his feet. "I think I know somewhere you'd get a really good night's sleep," he said. "You can tell me all about your adventures on the way."

So they walked, and they talked. At least, Jimmy talked and, apart from the occasional "What's that?" and the more frequent "You're having me on," Obegarde listened.

THIRTY-SEVEN

ELSEWHERE in the city, Duke Modeset was nodding off to sleep in his new room, when the window rattled. He turned over and tugged on the mangy rag that the innkeeper had assured him was a blanket.

A wolf howled, and the window rattled.

Modeset frowned, opened one eye, and peered over the edge of the blanket. Outside, the twin moons kept up their nighttime vigil. He couldn't see anything beyond the barrier, so, hugging his knees for warmth, he tried to drift off again.

An owl hooted, and the windows rattled.

It's that rotten bastard of an innkeeper, he thought. I bet there was a wedge for that window and he's had it removed . . . out of spite.

He sat up in bed and fixed his gaze on the glass as

the downtime rains began their vigorous bombardment of the city.

The window rattled.

Modeset sighed, leaped out of bed, and padded across the room. He didn't know what he expected to see, but it'd be fair to say that a vampire hanging from the gutter probably wouldn't have made his top ten.

Inconceivable, he thought. Forty-seven rooms and he's still gone and bloody found me.

The window was opened, and Obegarde barreled into the room. He did a neat little forward roll onto the floorboards, stood up, patted himself down, then spun around. Modeset thought he looked bigger in the half-light of the moons.

"Hello again," Obegarde said, not unpleasantly.

"Yes, indeed," said Modeset. "Good of you to visit. Er . . . how's everything going?"

Obegarde shrugged. "So-so," he said. "Nice room, this. Classy furniture."

"Yes, indeed," said the duke. "I expect you're wondering how I persuaded the innkeeper to part with it?"

"No," said Obegarde, taking a seat on the edge of the bed. "Actually, I was wondering why you didn't open the window sooner."

Modeset smiled humorlessly. "Now just look here: I've said I'll go and see this Vrunak chap. What more do you want?"

"I just wanted to tell you what I've found out."

Modeset folded his arms. He looked nonplussed. "I thought you didn't want me to stick my nose in," he said. "And then, as I recall, you almost broke it."

"Yeah, okay, but you might as well help now you're involved."

"What? I'm not involved! Not one bit."

Obegarde straightened himself up. He was well over six feet tall and, as far as Modeset could see, his wide chest didn't contain one ounce of flab.

"You're involved because I say you're involved," he began. "If you wanted to stay out of the case, you shouldn't have broken into the warehouse."

Modeset threw up his arms. "I didn't break into the warehouse, you idiot! I already told you what happened."

"Mmm. A likely story, and you're still going to Vrunak's house tomorrow. Now, listen—oh! I almost forgot."

Obegarde hurried over to the window, stuck his head outside, and motioned down toward the street. A few minutes later, a figure fell, puffing and wheezing, through the window and onto the floor of the room.

Obegarde gave Modeset a friendly grin. "I believe you know Jimmy Quickstint," he said.

When the duke had stopped shouting, Obegarde proceeded to tell him about Lopsalm, the second coming of Doiley, the missing book, and Jimmy's involvement with the barrowbird. Modeset eventually got to sleep at a quarter to seven.

THIRTY-EIGHT

IN THE FRONT GARDEN of a small cottage on Royal Road, a bush rattled in an extremely suspicious manner.

Jimmy Quickstint, who had circled the building twice, leaped over the low front wall to crouch beside the bush.

"There's nobody about," he said. "The kitchens are deserted, and I've had a squint in all the windows on the first floor. Why don't you just go and knock?"

Modeset stuck his head out of the biggest bush. "This is a very delicate matter," he said. "I'd thank you not to interfere beyond surveillance suggestions."

"It's up to you, Duke Modeset. I'm just trying to help."

"Well, don't."

Modeset was getting sick and tired of Jimmy. He'd already sent Flicka back to the inn because of her constant nagging—now he had to put up with the gravedigger's irritating chatter.

Jimmy yawned. "At least you can tell Obegarde we've checked the place out," he said. "There's obviously no one here."

"Please be quiet."

"Fine, fine."

Modeset got to his feet and stepped out of the bush, shoving the gravedigger aside. He marched up the garden path and hammered on the door.

"Mr. Vrunak? Mr. Vrunak! My name is Modeset. I wondered if I could have a quick chat with you."

Nothing.

Modeset put an ear to the door and listened, but he couldn't hear any movement from within.

"Kick it down," Jimmy urged. "No one'll hear."

"Shh! There must be another way."

"What d'you mean? A key under the welcome mat?"

Modeset looked down. There was no welcome mat. "Probably not," he admitted. "I'll try the flowerpot instead."

He reached down and lifted the pot, but there was nothing underneath it. He then tried running a hand under the wooden overhang at the foot of the door, working a finger into the keyhole and, finally, trying to get his fingernails around the edge of a fractured pane.

"Pity," said Jimmy, when he'd given up. "Full marks for effort, though."

Modeset shrugged. "Well, I've done what he asked me to do," he said, knowing deep down that it wouldn't be enough. "What more can he reasonably expect? It's not my fault if the man's not in."

"Exactly. We *should* go; I mean, we can hardly wait here all day."

"That's right! I'm not waiting around like some . . . peasant. Vrunak's out; well that's just too bad. Obegarde can come back when it's dark; do the job himself."

"Yep. Sounds fair."

"Right."

"Let's be off to meet him, then. Shall we?"

"Fine."

"Great."

The duke headed back up the garden path, Jimmy in tow. They were passing a dense thicket when Modeset tripped on a crack in the paving stones. He went down hard, and Jimmy, who hadn't managed to anticipate anything from the Dafisful incident onward, landed in a crumpled heap beside him.

Modeset groaned. He was bruised, his pride still ached, and he felt awful.

He tried to get to his feet, but Jimmy, suddenly alert, dragged him back down again and pulled him off the path. They rolled over one another before Modeset wrestled an arm free.

"Let go! What's with you?"

"Shh . . . there's someone coming."

Still flat to the ground, the duo watched as Vrunak's gate creaked open. A straggly and bedraggled man stepped into the garden, closed the gate behind him, and carried on up the path.

"It's the gnome from last night," Jimmy whispered. Mixer had reached Vrunak's front door, where he made straight for the flowerpot. When the key was found to be missing, he looked both ways and then flew into a rage, shaking his fists at the windows, kicking the door, and cursing Vrunak's name in a variety of different languages. Modeset thought that he heard the words "treacherous old git" mentioned more than once.

Eventually the gnome seemed to come to a decision and made his way around the side of the cottage.

"Should we try and capture him, d'you think?" Modeset ventured.

"Nah, I doubt we could. I know *I* couldn't."

Modeset looked affronted. "Speak for yourself, coward," he snapped. "I've had one fight already this week, so I—"

"Did you win?"

"Um . . . yes, sort of. In fact, the other chap didn't get a single blow in."

"Really? You're that good?"

"No, actually I ran away before he could react. Now, come on!"

The duke nodded toward the house, but his determination was interrupted.

"Oi!" Jimmy whispered. "Get down! He's comin' back."

Mixer, apparently unsuccessful in his quest to gain an illicit entrance to the cottage, emerged from the side of the building and stomped back up the path. When he reached the gate he took one last look at the house, spat on the ground, and headed off along Royal Road.

"We could follow him," said Jimmy doubtfully.

Modeset looked astonished. "Follow him? In order to achieve what, exactly?"

The gravedigger shrugged. "To see where he goes, of course. Why else would you follow somebody?"

"No," snapped Modeset. "I've got a much better idea. We split up, and *you* go after the gnome. Then you can come and find me at the inn."

"Why me?"

"You suggested it."

"So?"

"Just get a move on. Quick, before you lose him."

THIRTY-NINE

IT WAS EARLY EVENING in Dullitch, and the Diamond Clock on Crest Hill struck six.

Flicka, who had been sent onto the old, half-rotted balcony of the inn to watch out for Jimmy Quickstint, whistled a tune that provoked jeers from the weary market traders.

The innkeeper had guided Modeset into the basement of the Steeplejack Inn to wake Obegarde.

The duke sat on the bottom step of the basement staircase, fidgeting nervously and trying to keep his eyes off the coffin on which the loftwing had placed his early-evening pick-me-up; freshly squeezed beetroot juice.

"Thins the blood," he explained, when he saw Modeset's expression. "Have to keep healthy, don't you?"

Modeset shifted his buttocks to the top of a small wine barrel, but after a few minutes, looked about ready to give up and sit on the floor instead.

"So we're waiting on Jimmy," said Obegarde, savoring the juice with poorly concealed glee. Modeset had already filled him in on their expedition to Vrunak's house. "I've been researching the Grinswood," Obegarde continued, "and I fear we don't know the half of it, yet."

"Oh?"

"According to Jimmy, the barrowbird said it was a servant of the forest. That would also make it a servant of the Dark Trinity. 'Watchers,'" Obegarde explained, holding up a hand to stop Modeset interrupting. "Those that make sure everything stays as it is, more or less."

"Okay. And these watchers sent the bird when Jimmy's friend took the lizards, correct?"

"As far as I can make out, yes. But the point is, this all started up because our city's lunatic fringe group wanted 'em; we now know *why*."

There was a knock on the basement door, and Flicka poked her head around it. "A friend of yours," she said.

Jimmy staggered into the basement.

"Any luck?" said Obegarde, offering the gravedigger some beetroot juice, which he quite rightly refused.

"Yeah, he went home," Jimmy said. "Lives in a hovel west of the palace; a right old slum. I've seen better windows in a doll's house. Rump Lane, it's called. I waited till he went out before I came back. Maybe we can search the place."

Obegarde got to his feet. "Right. Who's with me?"

No one made a sound.

"I'll assume that's just myself and the duke, then." He glared at Modeset, who looked about ready to explode and then simmered down considerably.

"I'm up for it," said Flicka.

Jimmy realized he'd have to go, too, and groaned.

FORTY

RUMP LANE was one of the first roads to be built when Dullitch had laid its foundations on the ash-lands of Illmoor. Now, more than two hundred years later, it looked about the same.

"What a dump," said Obegarde.

"Absolute abomination," said Modeset.

"Used to rent a little place along here," Jimmy muttered. "It was all right. Bit of damp in the walls, but nothing worth condemning it over."

Obegarde put a finger to his lips. "I'm going in first," he said. "Just in case our friendly neighborhood gravedigger got it wrong, and Mixer's still home. The rest of you can wait here until I give the all clear."

They watched as the investigator walked over to the door and gripped the brass door handle. There was a brief pause, and then he disappeared inside. Seconds later he came flying backward out of one of the ground-floor windows. He had a gnome on top of him.

Flicka and Modeset rolled their eyes in sync.

The battle landed on the cobbles. After taking a few minor blows, Obegarde threw the gnome into a pile of rubbish bins and followed up his offensive with a well-aimed boot.

"I hate this guy," he said, panting as he pulled the unconscious gnome onto his feet. "I absolutely, unutterably, one hundred percent hate him. Jimmy, can you give me a hand getting him to the militia? He's got a nasty habit of giving me the slip."

Jimmy nodded, and hurried over to help.

"We'll meet you at the palace in one hour; get this mess sorted out," Obegarde called.

Modeset made to enter the hovel, then stopped and put a hand on Flicka's shoulder. "You stay here and watch for the militia," he commanded. "We've got until Obegarde gets to the guardhouse to search the place; after that, it'll be crawling with the district's finest."

FORTY-ONE

THE AIR in the hovel was musty.

"I'm up here," called Flicka from the top of the staircase. She'd abandoned her sentry post at the front door for a preferred position in the attic. It still afforded a fine view of the road, and she could search at the same time.

"Okay," Modeset shouted back. "Tell me if you find anything."

"Sure."

"Right."

Modeset stepped through a low door and looked around with unconcealed distaste at the room beyond.

The kitchen, like the rest of the hovel, was a threadbare affair. Rats congregated in the corner of the room, and Modeset was sure he could see a vole in the bargain.

The only decent piece of furniture in the room, as far as he could tell, was an aging iron stove that looked as though it might have value as scrap metal. It looked a little out of place and, Modeset was sure, a little out of sync with the wall. He stepped over to the dresser, hunkered down, leaned a shoulder against it, and, after several attempts, moved it aside. The wall sported several deep cracks. Modeset saw something wedged in the largest of these, and reached inside to pull it out. When he finally managed to wrench the obstacle free, he discovered it was in fact a book, and it weighed a ton.

He struggled over to the table and dropped the volume down with a spine-juddering smack.

"What was that?" shouted Flicka.

Modeset sighed.

"I've found a book," he bellowed back.

Groaning with effort, he heaved the book over and allowed it to slam down. On the cover etched in golden letters, were the letters:

EA   I   G
LE   N   S

Modeset squinted at the outline of the missing

letters, blinked, and looked again, but he still couldn't make any sense of the title. Then he rubbed the palm of his hand over the gold lettering and, losing patience, brushed a mountain of dust from the cover. Thus revealed, the writing read:

LEAVING
LEGENDS

Modeset frowned.

"*Leaving Legends*?" he said aloud.

"What's that?" asked Flicka. She emerged from the doorway and slumped down, out of breath, on a crooked stool beside the table.

"It's one of the Yowler holy books, or some close approximation. As I recall, they were always dropping leaflets into the guild; some rot about paying weekly for a copy if your earnings couldn't make the stretch."

"Except that this can't be a copy," Flicka commented, nodding at the tome. "I mean, look at it. It's got to be an original with all that braiding. I bet it was stolen. Nobody who lives *here* could afford a book like *that*."

"Hmm . . . as a matter of fact, it was stolen. From Karuim's Church, though by all accounts the theft was arranged."

Flicka scratched at a cut on her chin. "How do you know that?" she asked. "Obegarde?"

"Yes. He paid them a visit last night. Whatever this whole, twisted mess is all about, I'll make a fair bet it has more than a little to do with this book."

"You could be right, Lord M. What does it say?"

"I don't know. But I'm not going to read it here, that's for sure."

Modeset tried to pick up the book, but it was clearly too heavy to carry halfway across the city. Only the gods knew how a *gnome* had managed it.

He sighed, opened the top leaf, and began to read. After a few minutes, he looked up.

Flicka was staring expectantly at him. "What does it say?"

Modeset shrugged. "It's the usual religious drivel; starts off with some crazy prophet who's decided to resurrect Yowler, God of Scones—er—that might be Stones, I think. Yes, it is. Right, *anyway*, he tries to bring Yowler back to life by turning an entire town to stone."

"How?"

Modeset continued to turn the pages. "Erm . . . well, apparently, he took six special lizards called Batchtiki, and he put them into some kind of magic machine. There's a drawing of it here." He thought back to the hulking monstrosity in the shadows of Warehouse Six, but the illustration looked nothing like it.

"It's totally different," he muttered. "Totally. There's not one similarity in the design."

"I don't understand," Flicka said, watching the duke as if lipreading his words. "What are you talking about?"

Modeset pointed at the tome. "Obegarde found and destroyed a gigantic machine in one of the warehouses down at the harbor. It definitely had something to do with the Yowlers, because the church was logged as the receiver. I saw it with my own eyes, but it bore absolutely no resemblance to this thing in here." He jabbed a finger at the illustration. "*This* looks more like a lighthouse."

"That's because it *is* a lighthouse," Flicka ventured, peering over his shoulder. "If you look closely, there's an arrow next to the word 'machine.' You're on the wrong page."

The duke reached down and turned over a leaf.

On the new page was a picture that Modeset recognized immediately.

"That was it!" he exclaimed. "That was the thing in the warehouse!" His gaze fell to the writing beneath it.

"The lighthouse," Modeset continued, "having been powered by the glare of a Batchtiki-holding device, fired a charge of energy into the target—our machine at the warehouse—freezing everything within a five-dinat radius."

"What's a dinat?"

"Uh . . . about twenty miles," Modeset guessed.

Flicka looked suddenly aghast. "Th-they were going to turn the whole of Illmoor to stone!" she cried. "Those crazy, cretinous murderers! If Obegarde hadn't destroyed the machine—"

Modeset snapped his fingers for silence. "So," he began, brows knotting with the effort of deduction, "if this was the receptacle in the warehouse, and we can now reasonably assume that it was, then we no longer have that portion of the problem to worry about."

"There's a 'but' coming, isn't there?"

"I'm afraid so," Modeset warned. "Because it also says that the secondary machine is used to magnify the beam's resulting discharge. So one machine fires into the other, which magnifies the beam and explodes. Now, even allowing for the destruction of its magnifier, we can comfortably assume that the remaining beam's strike would still take in all of Dullitch and a little more besides."

"B-b-but that means we're all going to get tur—"

"All it means, *Flicka*, is that we need to find the primary machine. Pronto."

As the girl's smile froze, the duke read on, turning pages with increasing fervor.

"Ha! Here is where it gets interesting," he said. "'Distance and Trajectories': according to Doiley's first law, the machines have to be at least seventy miles apart."

"That's an incredible distance," said Flicka, who'd excelled in geography during a brief stint in cartography school. "Especially since the whole of Illmoor is only eighty miles, north to south."

"Okay," said Modeset, eyeing her carefully. "For the sake of argument, let's say that's right. You're good at geography, yes?"

"Yes," Flicka replied confidently. "So?"

"Well, what's at the other end of the continent?"

"Sorry?"

"Well, Dullitch occupies the southernmost point of eastern Illmoor, right?"

"Right."

"So, is there a town in the extreme north, past Grinswood?"

Flicka's face creased as she tried to recall the outline of the big wall-mounted map in the chief cartographer's office, but it was Modeset who answered his own question.

"Plunge!" he exclaimed. "Plunge is the northernmost town on the continent. Arrrgh!"

Flicka nearly jumped out of her skin. She gawped at the duke, who suddenly looked as if he were about to kill someone.

"What's wrong?" she said dubiously.

"Plunge falls within the jurisdiction of Fogrise," snapped Modeset. "My land!"

"Well, not technically *yours*, Lord M," Flicka pointed out. "At least not anymore: those old boundaries haven't existed for years! Besides, it's *miles* away from Fogrise."

"Yes, but it's still *my* land, my birthright, and it's as though they're firing a deadly beam from my back garden to destroy Dullitch! It's the principle of the thing! I'd feel responsible!" Modeset let out a long, depressed sigh. "What am I going to do?"

"Stop them from turning us all to stone?" Flicka hazarded. "It's just an idea, but— What? What did I say?"

Suddenly a light flickered in the duke's eyes, as if he'd been sitting in a corner for years and someone had just remembered to plug him in. Destiny beckoned. It told Modeset, in the confines of his head, that the time had come to take a stand, to do something truly heroic.

"C'mon, Flicka," he snapped. "We're going to avert a catastrophe. Your first, my second."

"Okay, Lord M. What're we going to do?"

"Well, *I'm* going to begin by reading this book from cover to cover, and then we're going back to the Steeplejack to fetch my battle attire. After that, I need to speak with my cousin."

"Are we going to get Pegrand?"

"Yes, among other things; now, keep a watch for those guards while I catch up on some history!"

FORTY-TWO

ISCOUNT CURFEW WAS surprised to see his cousin march into the palace throne room wearing a full suit of Fogrise armor. To increase the level of bewilderment (made evident by the shocked gasps of the royal bodyguards lurking in the shadows of the room), Modeset saluted.

"Apologies for the disturbance, my lord," he said. "But Dullitch is in grave danger, and I feel I owe it to the city to warn you."

Curfew licked his lips. For some reason the duke's renewed strength of voice concerned him.

"Um . . . grave danger, you say? Any chance you could be a little more specific?"

"A plot is underway—"

"Yes, I'm quite awa—"

"—to resurrect a dark god."

Curfew paused, lowered his hand. "Oh—" was all he could manage.

"This resurrection," Modeset continued, "may involve the people of Dullitch being turned to stone."

Curfew swallowed a few times and steepled his fingers. "You have proof of this, I assume?" he said unsteadily. "Such accusations are fruitless without—"

"Eyewitnesses can be provided later. Right now my needs are great. If I'm to stop this plot I will require a mage of some considerable skill to teleport a small company to Plunge."

A look of sudden, terrible recognition settled on the viscount's face. "Plunge," he said slowly. "Of course."

"Well, do you have a mage or don't you?"

"Yes, I mean, no! Absolutely not! Magic is outlawed in Dullitch, as you are well aware. I can, however, provide you with—"

"Horses simply won't make the journey in time, and I don't know anyone with a dragon."

Curfew got to his feet. "I'm not supplying you with magic unless I'm absolutely one hundred percent satisfied that a definite threat is posed to the city."

"Very well," Modeset agreed, leaning across the viscount's marble desk and staring him directly in the eye. "A beam comprised of the glare of several Batchtiki lizards is to be fired from a small machine through a sorcery-fueled lighthouse lens into the sun. The resulting beam *was* going to hit a specially constructed magnifier in Dullitch. Now, as I understand, the receptacle has been destroyed—"

"Yes, entirely."

"But that does not discount the fact that a beam will be fired and, though the resulting range will undoubtedly be reduced, I feel certain the malevolent group involved will inflict many, many deaths with it. Satisfied?"

Before Curfew could question him further, the duke stepped forward and placed both hands flat on the desktop. "Now," he began, eyeing the bodyguards who had begun to creep from the shadows. "Do you have a mage in the building or not?"

The viscount held up a hand. "Yes . . . very well."

The guards receded.

"I do hope you know what you're doing, cousin," Curfew warned.

Modesest took a step back and saluted again.

"How many men are you taking with you?" the viscount prompted.

"Three, my lord," said Modeset confidently. "And one woman."

FORTY-THREE

MANY MILES AWAY from the palace, in a great lighthouse atop the tiny town of Plunge, the Lark paced back and forth before a wide window that looked out upon the sea.

"Well," she said, not bothering to turn when she heard the door creak open. "Was our little experiment a success?"

"Yes, mistress," said Moors, trying to control his excitement with a nervous laugh. "But I'm afraid Edwy got a little carried away."

"Oh?" The Lark twirled around, her robed arms folded in annoyance. "Do explain."

Moors hauled himself farther into the room, practically blocking out all light from the passage behind him.

"Well, I *changed* the villagers exactly as you said,

mistress: slowly, one at a time. But Edwy started trying to do two at once, then three and four, and—"

"I get the picture," the Lark snapped. "So we now have the entire town under wraps, do we?"

Moors managed a sheepish nod. "I'm afraid so, mistress. I did *warn* him not to go too far, but you know Edwy, mistress, he doesn't listen."

The Lark shook her head. "No," she echoed quietly. "He'll pay for that. Still, no matter; the test can be considered a success."

"Yes, mistress," Moors bleated. "Is there anything else we should be doing?"

The Lark nodded quickly. "There is. Fetch Edwy. We're going to accelerate our plans a little. Dullitch falls tonight!"

FORTY-FOUR

THE CELLAR BENEATH Dullitch Palace was in an absolute uproar.

"Are you sure this man's playing with a full deck?" Modeset demanded, pointing across the room at the viscount's resident (and highly classified) sorcerer.

It was no wonder Curfew kept Wrickshaw Muldoon in the basement. The old man had a face like the first actor in a play to forget his lines. He was impossibly ancient, excruciatingly wizened, and uncomfortably shortsighted.

"You," he announced, suddenly thrusting out an arm. "Do not dare speak ill of my powers."

Modeset rolled his eyes. "I'm over this way."

"I knew that! I was just testing your reflexes."

"Ha! Are any of you listening to this rubbish?

We'd have more luck being teleported by an incontinent whippet."

"Can we please get on?" said Curfew, holding up a hand for silence. "Good. Now, can everyone intent on saving our city please step into the circle of voluntary transportation?"

There was a lot of mumbling, and several city dignitaries secreted themselves in remote corners of the cellar. Modeset remained, accompanied by Flicka and Pegrand Marshall, his newly released manservant. Obegarde also occupied the inside of the circle, stepping aside to admit the reluctant figure of Jimmy Quickstint.

"Why am I doing this again?" the gravedigger asked, then muttered under his breath when nobody provided an answer.

"Very good," Curfew applauded. "Now, are you all ready to go to Plunge?"

"Yes."

"Yeah."

"S'pose so."

"Do we have any choice?"

Curfew beamed. "Superb! Now, if you would be so kind, Mr. Muldoon?"

The sorcerer stepped forward, raised one withered arm, and promptly turned one of the skulking officials into a herring.

The group, as one, swallowed. Modeset looked daggers at the old man.

"Does he have any idea what he's doing?"

"Please control your temper, cousin. I'm sure Mr. Muldoon was merely warming up, isn't that right, Wrickshaw?"

Muldoon nodded, gave a lopsided smile, and began to concentrate again. A few moments later, Modeset disappeared in a puff of smoke. Flicka coughed and spluttered in the resulting cloud, and Obegarde had to thrust out an arm in order to block Jimmy's sudden bid for escape.

Pegrand gasped and stumbled in bewildered awe toward the place where Modeset had been standing. He hadn't quite reached the spot, when he too winked out of existence. Flicka was the third to evaporate, but then a lengthy pause ensued.

"What's the problem?" Obegarde bellowed. Jimmy looked faintly hopeful.

Curfew strode over to the old sorcerer and leaned in close; whispers were exchanged.

"There is no problem, I assure you," said the viscount calmly. "Mr. Muldoon simply requires a few moments in which to regain his energy."

The loftwing sighed. "Can't he just get on with it?"

Curfew swallowed. "Mr. Obegarde, you must understand that if our sorcerer is not able to recuperate his powers, he might not be able to send you to Plunge in one piece."

"We don't have time," Obegarde said. "I'll take the risk."

"Fantastic," Jimmy mumbled. "I bet I lose all my favorite bits."

PART THREE

THE

FIGHT FOR PLUNGE

FORTY-FIVE

PLUNGE BAY STOOD on the northern
fringe of Illmoor, at a point where the Grinswood
gave way to the Mountains of Mavokhan. In the past,
it *had* been a picturesque little town full of fat,
friendly fishermen and their bloated, odious wives.
It *had* been a place where the aristocrats of Dullitch
sent their children during the height of summer,
and a place where retired wizards came to settle
down and raise magically inept sons and dizzy
daughters who always got into the kind of trouble a
wand couldn't fix.

Plunge Bay *had* been all these things and more
besides. Now, however, it was . . .

"Empty, milord; the town's a complete morgue."

Pegrand Marshall, standing in the middle of the
street with his blunderbuss at the ready, squinted up

to the roof of the nearest house to try and determine whether Duke Modeset had heard him. Flicka was still materializing at the far end of the street. Jimmy Quickstint and Obegarde were, as yet, nowhere to be seen.

"It's empty!" he bellowed again, just in case.

"I heard you the first time, Pegrand," said a voice beside him.

Modeset shimmered into view, his fully-armed form becoming a little less hazy as the materialization spell wore off. Evidently, his own journey through enchantment had been somewhat less smooth than that of his companions.

"I don't like it," he said. "It's not right. A whole town can't just disappear. Have a look inside some of those houses, will you?"

The manservant hurried over to one of the doors and hammered on it, using its ornamental brass knocker. When he got no reply, he slipped inside and reappeared minutes later, sporting a worried grin.

"There is a woman in there, milord," he said. "But she's been turned to stone."

Pegrand tried rapping on another door farther down the street. To his surprise, Obegarde answered it.

"Found the loftwing, milord! He came down in the butcher's . . ."

Thunder rumbled off to the east, a distant echo of sound. Somehow, it made the vacancy of Plunge seem even more forbidding. Doors creaked open in the wind and dust gathered on neglected panes.

Flicka rushed up to join the duke as she fiddled with her clothes in a distracted manner; she felt sure that the spell had distorted the fabric. Obegarde looked even worse; the investigator kept shaking his head and had apparently lost the power of speech in the bargain.

Pegrand hunched his shoulders and rubbed his wrists.

"What're we dealing with here, milord?" he asked, staring off into the distance.

"A difficult prospect," Modeset answered. "But at least we know we're in the right place. Presumably, the unfortunate population of Plunge has been exposed to the glare of the lizards as some sort of preparative experiment for the turning to stone of Dullitch."

"We need some sort of weapon," Obegarde piped up, peering around the empty streets. "Something bigger than that blunderbuss: a siege cannon, maybe. Something major . . ."

They watched as he disappeared down a side alley, only to reemerge from the mouth of a second, some distance along the road. He beckoned to them, then suddenly veered left.

"Where's he off to?" said Modeset, nudging Pegrand in the ribs to shake the manservant from his reverie.

"Dunno, milord. I'll try and get his attention." Pegrand flung up his arms and started shouting.

"Will you shut up, Pegrand! You'll alert the Yowlers! We'll catch up to him, okay?"

"Right, milord. Sorry."

"Where's young Jimmy got to?"

"Don't think he's arrived yet, milord. Flicka's disappeared as well."

"Oh, for goodness' sake, where is everybody? We've only been here five minutes and we're already a bloody shambles!"

"Quiet, milord! You'll alert the Yowlers."

Modeset cast a sharp glance at Pegrand, then clipped him round the ear.

FORTY-SIX

"S ORRY, LORD M," Flicka said when the duke and Pegrand had caught up with her on the first floor of one of the fishermen's cottages. "But I had to get a closer look at the peninsula and I just knew one of these rooms would overlook the bay. I haven't seen Jimmy yet. I hope the spell didn't go wrong or anything. . . ."

Pegrand shrugged and began to rummage through the cupboards. "No weapons here," he said eventually, and ripped off one of the doors for good measure. "Have to rely on me and my blunderbuss, milord."

"May the gods have mercy," said Obegarde, conquering the stairs of the cottage and leaning half-heartedly against the door frame.

"Find anything?"

"No," said the loftwing sulkily. "Not so much as a knuckle-duster."

"Great. You all right, milord?"

Modeset, still taken aback by the stone statue of a small boy beside the window, didn't reply. He took a moment to mentally rewind what Flicka had said earlier.

"What peninsula?" he said to her, when he'd finished his thinking process.

"The one with the lighthouse on the end," said Flicka, gesturing out of the window toward a towering column just visible in the distance. "I noticed it from the end of the road, while you were talking. There's a localized storm there, which is odd. It's a little *too* localized if you ask me."

"*Sorcery*," said Modeset, eyes narrowing. "Our friends from the church, no doubt."

Pegrand marched over to the window and squinted out. "Should we go in guns blazing, milord?"

"No, thank you, Pegrand. That will not be necessary until after you've learned how to operate the weapon you're carrying."

The manservant frowned. "How do you mean, milord?"

"Well, for starters, the barrel is pointing *toward* your chest. . . ."

Pegrand glanced down. "Oh, will you look at that? So it is."

". . . Meaning that if you'd heard a noise on the way up here and had, in reaction, pulled the trigger, Flicka and I would now be scraping sections of your rib cage from the walls."

"Point taken, milord."

"Jolly good. Now, I want you to hand the blunderbuss over to Obegarde."

"Oh, do I have to?"

"Immediately and without argument."

"But why?"

"Because, dear friend, I have to focus my mind on defeating the enemies of Dullitch, and I'm going to find that extremely difficult if I have to keep looking over my shoulder to make sure you don't accidentally blow my head off with your six seconds of ballistic experience. Okay?"

Pegrand mumbled something under his breath and shoved the gun toward Obegarde, who accepted it with no particular show of emotion.

"Now," Modeset continued, "we're going to make for the lighthouse."

"I don't fancy walking into the jaws of death without good reason, milord," said Pegrand.

The duke sighed.

"I don't have time to argue," he said pleasantly. "Suffice it to say, old friend, that if I'm going, then so are you."

FORTY-SEVEN

ODESET AND COMPANY were on
their way over to the lighthouse when Pegrand suddenly barked an announcement.

"The saber! The silver saber!"

Modeset and Flicka froze; Obegarde took a deep
breath.

"What?" the duke asked, bewildered.

"The sacred silver saber."

"What *are* you talking about?"

"The sacred silver saber of Bowlcock, milord!"

Modeset frowned at his manservant. "Bowlcock,"
he said slowly. "You mean—"

"The first duke of Dullitch," Pegrand confirmed
with a sudden grin. "The greatest warrior who ever
walked the land. On his deathbed, he donated his
sacred silver saber, the weapon that'd never failed

him, to a museum in Plunge! It must still be here somewhere!"

"How do you know all that?" asked Modeset, aghast at the possibility that the final movements of his greatest ancestor had escaped him.

Pegrand looked nonplussed. "I read it in the *Collected Histories of Dullitch*, milord. Volume Six, I believe. If we can find the museum, we'll find the saber."

"I don't understand," Flicka chimed in. "Why would we want it?"

Pegrand gasped. "Why would we want it? The sacred silver saber of Bowlcock? We'd *want* it because it's a charmed weapon. Bowlcock never lost a single fight with it. He took on dragons, wyverns, trolls, giants, and an army of greenskins. It's got—"

"Historical significance," Modeset finished. "Yes, I can appreciate that. Destiny has its wily ways. Besides, in a town this size, it shouldn't take too long to find the museum."

Obegarde made a sucking sound with his cheeks. "I'll wait here," he said, "but do remember that lives may well be at stake. We haven't got all day!"

FORTY-EIGHT

THREE AND A HALF hours of frantic searching had laid bare the Plunge treasury, gold reserve, bakery, butchers, merchants' tenement, armory, food stores, and blacksmiths' forge; not to mention fourteen private houses.

All the while, Obegarde stood in the town square, tapping his foot and kicking the occasional wall.

"I don't believe this," said Pegrand, sighing and stamping his foot on the dusty floor of yet another food store. "They must have eaten like rabid animals."

"It's a pity we haven't got a map of some kind," said Modeset.

"There's a place we've missed."

"Yes, a map!" Pegrand agreed, ignoring the brief

interruption. "There would have to be one in the town hall."

"Town hall's full of statues," said Modeset dismissively. "There must've been a big meeting or something. I assume the villagers were all caught unawares; it's like Medusa's garden in there."

Modeset frowned suddenly. "What do you mean, 'a place we missed'?" he demanded, turning to Flicka. She was standing with her arms folded, gazing nonchalantly out to sea.

"Well?" Modeset prompted. "What place?"

"A big building with brass dogs outside, right next to the town gates. We've walked past it five times; I have been trying to tell you but nobody seems to be listening."

"Very well," said Modeset, stung by the tiny flicker of embarrassment he always felt whenever he looked directly at her. "We'll check it out at once, but I prefer to take the back alley. I don't think I could bear walking past Obegarde after his last outburst."

The door to the Plunge Museum was locked. Modeset eventually had to break a window in order to gain entrance.

Inside, the building was dark and shadowy. Glass

display cases crowded the walls and a heavy candelabra hung down from a grand mosaic ceiling.

"I'll start on the left," said Modeset. The others mumbled in agreement and wandered off toward various cases huddled in bleak corners of the room.

The first case, Modeset noted with no great interest, contained the skull of Baron Huckstep, a little-known retainer of the Plunge crest who had helped rescue the town from a great dragon back in the Dual Age. It was in two separate pieces.

Next up, after the vertebrae of several infamous (and rather less than respectable) marquesses, came the legendary Tarnish Helmet that had almost saved Sir Cuffock from the Witches of Rinstare. Judging by the shape of it—an inverted L—the margin of survival had been pretty narrow (evidently, unlucky for some).

Modeset sighed. He found himself wondering what the people of Dullitch would keep as a reminder of *him*. A nose hair, perhaps, or some earwax? No, he reflected, it would probably be something like "the gold tooth of Duke Modeset" with a footnote declaring, "the only thing of any value we found on him." He scowled at the thought and moved on.

He was studying a metal clasp belonging to some long-forgotten king, when a gasp from Pegrand disturbed his concentration.

"What is it, man?" he called over.

"It's this bloke, here. They've only got his what-sit on a plinth!"

The duke sighed. "I don't want to know, Pegrand."

"His whatsit, though, milord! His actual *whatsit*."

"Yes, so you said."

"He must've been pretty successful with the women for 'em to remember him like that."

"Yes, I'm sure. Now, please forget about it and continue your search." He turned to look behind him. "Any luck yet, Flicka?"

The aide shook her head and mumbled neg-atively.

Modeset returned his attention to the line of cases he'd been perusing. Then he stopped short.

"Pegrand," he said slowly. "You told us about Lord Bowlcock's generous donation of the sacred silver saber to Plunge Museum, do you remember?"

The manservant was quick to frown. "Of course I do, milord."

Modeset swallowed and tried to hide the unease

in his voice. "Well, would you like to know what *else* the great lord donated to the museum?"

"Um . . . yes. What?"

"Himself."

"Sorry, milord?"

"Lord Bowlcock," Modeset repeated, pronouncing each word with extreme care, "donated himself, along with the super saber you were talking about."

"It's there? The saber's actually there?"

"Oh, yes. In fact, he's still holding it. Only he doesn't look all that keen to let it go."

Pegrand hurried over, Flicka trailing behind him.

The skeleton beyond the glass barrier was still clutching the silver saber with both hands. It looked ancient in the true sense of the word, not merely long decrepit but well and truly worm-ridden; so off the coil as to be almost nonexistent.

Pegrand reached out to touch the glass, but Modeset stayed his hand.

"Wait, man! What if it's cursed?"

"Cursed, milord? What, Lord Bowlcock or the sword?"

"Both!"

"Well, of course it's up to you, milord," said the

manservant, stepping back. "But look at the luck we've had so far."

Modeset nodded. "Good point," he said. "I'll grab it, then, if you don't mind."

"Of course not, milord."

Pegrand and Flicka stood back as the duke looked around for something to throw at the case. Eventually, he settled on an old wooden stool behind the entrance doors.

The glass shattered.

"Right," Modeset announced. "Here goes nothing."

Mindful of the glass shards, he leaned in to the display case and began the difficult task of removing Lord Bowlcock's clasped fingers from the silver saber.

"I'd have thought that they'd just crumble away, milord," said Pegrand helpfully.

"Hmm . . . it seems not." In less than a minute, Modeset had resorted to applying pressure on the upper arm with his boot. "I certainly didn't expect this much resistance."

He gave one final wrench and staggered back, clutching not only the silver saber but Lord Bowlcock's arm as well.

"Damnation! Of all the luck!"

"Hold on, milord. I'll help you out, there."

Pegrand and Modeset played tug-of-war with the sword arm and saber for what seemed like an age.

"Flicka!" snapped the duke. "Get over here and help us, will you?"

Flicka joined in, but to no avail.

"Very well," Modeset said, face flushed with a mixture of embarrassment and fury. "We'll leave the arm on; I'll use the saber as it is."

"You can't do that, Lord M," Flicka warned. "You'll do yourself an injury."

"She's right there, milord," added Pegrand. "Every time you swing it round, the elbow'll catch you on the chin. It'll be like fighting two opponents at once."

Modeset raised the saber and, ignoring the arm that dangled down from it, smiled proudly.

"Pegrand," he began. "This is my ancestor, my flesh and blood. He will not impede my victory!"

He took an experimental swing with the sword and yelped when its appendage almost took off his ear.

Obegarde, arriving at the museum just in time to witness the display, clicked his tongue and sighed deeply.

"When you've all quite finished running around this cement garden of a town, raiding food stores and perusing museums, do you think that there's even the slightest smidgen of a chance that you might accompany me to the lighthouse in an attempt to save the entire population of a certain city? You know, if it's not too much trouble?"

He made to leave, then turned and strode up to Flicka, depositing the blunderbuss in her hands. "You take this," he commanded. "I'm better off fighting the old-fashioned way."

FORTY-NINE

"THEY'RE COMING, mistress, they're coming!"

Edwy burst through the door to the top floor of the lighthouse, his breath almost failing him as he hurtled to a halt.

The Lark was preoccupied with her glare machine. "Mmm . . . who is?" she said distractedly.

"City folk, mistress! There's a group of them."

The Lark released her grip on the machine and spun around, her attention suddenly seized. "Inconceivable! Who are they?"

"One of them is the man I saw in Dullitch; he came to the temple to speak with Lopsalm."

"The wretched loftwing. Hmm . . . that would make sense. I thought I felt an invasive little mind trying to read my thoughts. Still, he got here exceptionally fast, which is troubling—"

"Yes, mistress. Mixer failed you, mistress."

"Of course he did; I'm surrounded by incompetents. What about the other members of this raiding party? Who are they?"

"I don't know, mistress; I can't quite make them out. What should we do?"

"Nothing. You've done enough already."

Edwy bowed his head. "Yes, mistress."

"For now, I need you to take control of the machine. It's being primed, and the glare is being collected. Keep it aimed through the lighthouse lens, but do not release the beam until I return. That is *my* birthright."

Edwy bowed and took over at the reins of the machine. "What are you going to do, mistress?"

The Lark secured her hair in a ponytail and smiled cruelly. "I'm going to kill a vampire."

She turned and swept out of the room, calling behind her, "If Moors comes lumbering up here, tell him to guard the floor below."

"Yes, mistress. I will, mistress."

FIFTY

THE PENINSULA LEADING to Plunge Lighthouse was long and winding, and the approach offered much in the way of conveniently placed bushes. Modeset and company nipped from cover to cover as they neared the towering structure.

The storm that had been hovering over the lighthouse had diminished considerably, but an ethereal glow still warned of magical activity inside.

Modeset dashed straight to the door, giving an indication to Pegrand, who joined him, to kick at the door. Unfortunately, all they got was a dull thud. Even Obegarde's hardened boot couldn't penetrate the door.

"Flicka," Modeset said, turning abruptly on his heel. "The door, if you please."

Flicka nodded, looked along the barrel of the blunderbuss, and pulled the trigger.

Nothing happened.

"She's not doing it right," Pegrand said, snatching the weapon and re-aiming it. He pulled the trigger.

Nothing happened.

"Let me see that," Flicka snapped, yanking the weapon back. She turned it over a few times and sighed. "You can't fire it because it's not real."

"Eh?"

"What do you mean?"

She shrugged. "It's only the *model* of a blunder-buss. Where did you say you got it from?"

"That elf guard gave it to me," the manservant muttered, looking down at his feet. "You know, the one who his lordship assaulted—"

"Fantastic, Pegrand, and you didn't think this generous gift was a little odd?"

Modeset straightened up. "Right," he said, speaking with renewed authority. "I'm going to climb up to one of the lower windows and break through. Then I'll crawl inside, disarm the guards (assuming there are guards), run down, and let you all in. I'll need help getting up, though. Perhaps we can form a sort of human ladder. . . ."

Pegrand and Flicka both looked extremely doubtful.

"This is a joke," Obegarde warned. "I'll have no part of it."

"Please yourself."

"Oh, come *on*. There must be another way."

"As I said, Obegarde, please *yourself*. You're your own man."

Modeset disappeared around the base of the lighthouse. A few seconds later, he returned.

"It's far too high," he said. "Pegrand, you get dow—"

He was interrupted by a small clap of lightning and a sudden puff of smoke. Jimmy Quickstint winked into existence, hovered in midair for a few seconds, and then collapsed onto the ground beside the lighthouse.

"Where did you come from?" Pegrand demanded. "More to the point, where in the name of Urgumflux the Wormridden did you *go*?"

A strangely tortured smile appeared on the gravedigger's gormless face. "I think I got a bit stretched," he announced in a far-off voice. "In fact, it feels like only a bit of me is here."

"Yes," Flicka chirped. "You're right about

that. In fact, if I were you, I should go down to the village right now and find some clothes to put on."

Jimmy looked down, and gulped.

FIFTY-ONE

"PEGRAND, KEEP STILL down there!"

"Hold on, milord! I'm trying to get Flicka's foot off my shoulder."

"Don't do that, man! We'll all collapse!"

"But she's digging it in on purpose, milord!"

"I *am* not. It's Jimmy, he's buckling!"

"Well, what do you expect? This apron doesn't fit me! Besides, Obegarde keeps tickling my feet!"

Modeset stood at the top of the human tower, fingernails scratching for purchase on the pasty surface of the lighthouse wall. He was about an inch short of the ledge at the base of the lowest window.

"Pegrand, stand on tiptoe!"

"Arrgghhh!"

The human tower was raised a little, and Modeset's searching fingers found the ledge. He scrambled up and rolled inside the window. Behind him, the tower collapsed. Pegrand folded up and Flicka managed to roll, but Jimmy landed awkwardly and knocked himself unconscious.

Obegarde shook his head sadly. "Well, you can count the boy out. Look at him—he's stone cold!"

Flicka moved to kneel beside the gravedigger (who'd managed to acquire a baker's apron from one of the houses nearest the lighthouse) and cradled his head in her arms.

"Are you okay, Jimmy? Can you hear me?"

"He's all right," said Pegrand. "He's still breathing, you see?"

Flicka forced a weak smile. "He's been through a lot," she said. "Maybe we should leave him be. You lot go on, I'll stay here with him, make sure he's all right."

The manservant nodded. "See you around, then."

"Good luck," said Flicka. "Don't get turned to stone or anything."

"Yeah, right. We'll try not to."

Pegrand took one last look at the pale face of Jimmy Quickstint and made for the lighthouse door.

* * *

"Hello?"

Pegrand peered around the door of the light-house, swallowed, and stepped inside.

"Are you up there, milord?" he said, moving aside as Obegarde stepped across the threshold.

"No, I'm behind the door," said Modeset.

"Oh, I am sorry, sir. I thought you'd be at the top by now."

Modeset smiled humorlessly. Then he wrestled himself free from the gap between the wall and the door, and staggered to the foot of the stairs. The lighthouse was engulfed in a thick, forced silence; the kind that usually precedes an explosion. However, before Modeset could remark on this, a resounding click signaled the closing of a door at least three floors above them.

He glanced sideways at Pegrand and, finding no encouraging smile from that quarter, took a reluc-tant step forward and prepared to mount the spiral staircase.

"Well, here goes," he said. The manservant nod-ded in a way that indicated he'd be bringing up the rear from somewhere near Dullitch.

"I'm not sure if we should be doing this,

milord," whispered Pegrand. "I mean, this Lark's one of them magical types, right? So this is a job for a wizard, surely."

"In any other town, yes. But Plunge falls within the jurisdiction of Fogrise Keep and, therefore, it's a job for me."

"But you don't even like the place, milord."

"What has fondness got to do with it? Fogrise towns are my towns by inheritance. It's the principle of the thing."

"I suppose so. But, by that argument, what about the time when Wild Chives attacked Brimtown?"

Modeset sighed. "What about it?"

"You said the villagers could all burn."

Obegarde sniggered.

"Nonsense," Modeset snapped. "I would never encourage vandalism in the Fogrise communities."

"Eh? You gave 'em the money for torches, didn't you? And that siege cannon of theirs had 'sponsored by Modeset' along the side."

"Yes, well, those were very hard times, Pegrand. Back then we sold out to oppression. Now we're fighting for, for—"

"A sack of lizards," Obegarde interrupted. "Essentially."

"Well, yes, *essentially*." The duke took a moment to consider things. "Hardly seems worth all the effort, does it?"

The investigator shrugged. "Not sure; I've never gone much on morality. I suppose one way of looking at it would be to say that we're trying to save an endangered species as well as a city. That's assuming everything Jimmy told us about the bird is true."

"Yes, you're absolutely right! Onward and upward, as they say."

Modeset drew the sacred silver saber and hurried up the stairs, trying to keep Lord Bowlcock's arm tucked under his own. Pegrand waited until he was out of sight and then followed sheepishly after him, but Obegarde remained rooted to the spot. Something very interesting had caught his attention.

FIFTY-TWO

THERE WERE TWO doors on the first land-ing of the lighthouse. Saber drawn (literally) at arm's length, Modeset stood on the landing, glanc-ing nervously from one to the other. Eventually Pegrand padded up the last few stairs and almost collapsed. He leaned against the wall for support while he got his breath back.

"Oh, for goodness' sake, man," Modeset whispered. "When was the last time you took some exercise?"

Pegrand shrugged. "Dunno, milord," he man-aged. "I can't remember much before my eighth birthday."

"You mean you haven't taken any kind of exercise since you were eight?"

"Well . . ."

"Do you know how dangerous that is?"

"Not sure, milord. About as dangerous as tryin' to stop a mad priestess from turnin' a city to stone?"

"Yes, very amusing, Pegrand. We'll have to look into your fitness."

"If we survive this, you mean?"

"Exactly. Now, are you going to take the left- or the right-hand door?"

The manservant shrugged. "Er, well, seein' as you've got the saber, milord. I thought I might just wait out here on the landing."

"Okay, in that case we'll go in together. The question remains; left or right?"

Pegrand took a good long stare at each option. "I read somewhere that evil is always defined as the left-hand path, milord."

"Right it is, then."

"Hang about; isn't this woman we're after supposed to be evil?"

"Make your mind up, man! They'll have turned Dullitch to stone by the time we've put in an appearance!"

Modeset darted forward and put a shoulder to the left-hand door. When, after three or four charges, the door still hadn't given way, he turned the handle instead.

"Unlocked, milord! There's a turn up for the books."

Modeset gripped his shoulder in agony. "I really hate you, Pegrand."

"Ha! You're a fair old joker, milord."

"Yes . . . now, come on. Let's move."

"Right behind you, milord."

The manservant stepped aside to let his master go first, shivering with cold as Modeset used the edge of the saber to urge open the door. It creaked back on tired hinges.

The room beyond was unremarkable in structure. With no additional doors, one minuscule barred window, and no furniture to speak of, it felt like a prison cell. The only thing of any interest was the cage full of baby lizards nestling in the far corner.

Modeset's reaction was instinctive, if a little peculiar. He flung the arm 'n' saber wide, dropped onto his stomach, and buried his head in his hands.

"Look away, Pegrand!" he cried. "It's them! It's the Batchtiki! Look away quickly!"

"Oh, come on, milord. You don't honestly believe—"

Silence.

Modeset moaned and hammered his fists on the

floor. Then, expecting the worst, he raised his head, eyes tightly shut against the glares he could still feel harpooning him.

"Pegrand? Pegrand! Answer me now, man!"

Silence.

Modeset reached for his sword, grasped it by the arm, and began to pull himself around to face the door. Eventually, he opened his eyes.

The manservant had been frozen in midstep. His mouth formed a surprised "O" and his eyes were glazed.

Modeset fought to control his temper; any sudden outburst would invariably alert the machine operator on the roof.

Remembering the folklore passages in *Leaving Legends*, Modeset used his shining silver wrist guard to view the Batchtiki. The reflection showed him that there were five of them in the cage; all seemed impatient to escape.

Modeset got to his feet and, heaving Pegrand's statue onto his back, hurried from the room and slammed the door shut. Outside on the landing, he propped the manservant against the east wall and made for the opposite room, which fortunately turned out to contain a small armory.

FIFTY-THREE

THE SHAPE WAS SO slight that at first Obegarde thought he was seeing things. It started as a small orb, spinning in one corner of the ceiling, just below the first flight of the spiral staircase. Neither Modeset nor Pegrand had noticed it, but Obegarde's superior vision had picked up the glimmer immediately. Now, somewhat worryingly considering their intended ambush, it was flashing red and green.

Obegarde cursed, and was about to hunt around outside for a suitable stone to throw at it, when the globe suddenly began to grow. Descending as it swelled, the globe re-formed into the features of a sharp and extremely intimidating woman. She was attractive, raven-haired, and emanated a presence quite unlike any Obegarde had encountered before.

He tried to run, but his legs wouldn't move. He stood rooted to the spot as the facial image shimmered and expanded into an elfin figure, which emerged from the pool of light.

"Modeset!" Obegarde cried, fighting against his own inability to escape the paralysis brought on by the Lark. "Pegrand! Jimmy! Flicka! Anybody! Help me out, here!"

Somehow, the words became muffled as soon as they left his lips. He actually felt the sound reverberate and die before him. The reply, however, was not so impaired.

"The loftwing, I presume. Let us silence you first, shall we?"

The Lark stepped forward, mumbling unrepeatable syllables under her breath, and quite calmly closed a clawlike hand around his neck. She drove her other hand into his chest, and he felt fingernails like sharpened glass pierce his heart.

Obegarde threw punches and kicks that would have devastated a mountain troll, but still the Lark maintained her stranglehold, still she pierced his heart. He staggered backward, feeling the life drain from his body. Finally, in a last-ditch attempt to fight his way out, he tightened his jaw muscles and extended his fangs until they curved in a wide arc. Then he ceased his backward drive and darted forward, biting sharply into the Lark's exposed neck.

"Ahhhhhh!"

She screamed and stumbled back, but in doing so she closed her fist around the loftwing's heart. Clutching at the fresh wound in her neck, she yanked her arm from the vampire and fell against the wall.

Obegarde gave one last smile of satisfaction and collapsed in a heap on the floor.

Still grasping the bite on her neck, the Lark pushed herself from the wall. She gave the loftwing an experimental prod with her foot. He was dead.

"Interesting that the city's resistance should include a vampire," she said, as if the now silent Obegarde could still hear her. "How . . . quaint. Oh well, onward and upward."

She folded her dark cloak about her and promptly vanished in a puff of smoke.

FIFTY-FOUR

ARMED WITH A short bow, two throwing daggers, and Lord Bowlcock's arm and its trusty saber, Modeset negotiated the rest of the spiral staircase and found himself in a small passage with a ladder leading to a trapdoor in the roof. A repulsively obese man stood on guard duty. At least, he would have been on guard duty had he actually been awake. Heaven only knew how he'd managed to drag that gut up two hundred stairs, Modeset reflected.

He crept over to the man, took a few moments to consider how his ancestors might have tackled the situation, and pummeled him on the head with the hilt of a dagger. Then, groaning with the effort, he dragged the unconscious figure away from the base of the ladder before beginning his ascent.

There were muffled voices coming from the

other side of the trapdoor. Raising it a gnat's wing, Modeset heard snatches of conversation.

"Won't stay still, mistress!"

"Idiot! Just concentrate, will you?"

"S'not my fault, mistress! The little bugger keeps running between the tubes! Maybe we should fetch the rest of them, and then—"

"Don't be ridiculous! If you can't keep one of them in check, how on Illmoor do you envisage handling six?"

"Well, I thought . . . er . . . can't we follow the prophecy with one lizard?"

"No! The machine must be at full strength, and that requires the glare of no less than six!"

"But, mistress, the intruders—"

"Are pathetic incompetents. I can assure you, Edwy, I've dealt with the only one capable of any kind of offense. Now, just do as you're tol—"

Before the Lark could finish, the trapdoor flew open and Modeset erupted from within. Fueled by an uncharacteristic taste for battle that went far beyond simple heroism, he pitched both daggers at Edwy and let out a scream of victory when one of them caught the Yowler disciple just above the knee-cap. Edwy grabbed at his leg, gasped, and fainted.

"You?" cried the Lark. "Modeset, isn't it? The Great Duke of Rats! Ha-ha-ha-ha!" She took a step back and removed a glass sphere from the sleeve of her robe. Muttering an incantation under her breath, she flung the sphere toward Modeset, her eyes gleaming as it erupted into flame. The duke, still thinking on his feet, used the silver saber to field the sphere right back at her, his fist closed tightly around Bowlcock's fist on the handle.

The sphere exploded in the Lark's face with a subdued flare. As she staggered against the far wall, Modeset saw his chance and darted forward.

One thrust with the silver saber shattered the huge glass eye of the lighthouse. It was only as Modeset turned to take out the glare machine that he realized his mistake. The Lark should have been his priority.

Now he found himself face-to-face with the machine.

In the few seconds he'd taken to demolish the glass eye, the Lark had wheeled the machine around to face him. Somewhere in those tubular bowels, the Batchtiki was glaring. Its stare, reflected and magnified through a network of tiny mirrors, fired a ray directly at the duke.

This is it, he thought. I'm absolutely, positively, going to die.

He closed his eyes.

He swallowed.

He held his arms up over his head and crossed them.

Then it happened.

The Batchtiki's ray hit Modeset's shiny wrist guard and beamed back directly along its length. When the duke finally did pluck up enough courage to open his eyes, the machine had been turned to stone.

Silence reigned in the little room.

Modeset put a fingertip to his forehead and wiped away a bead of sweat.

"And let that be a lesson to you," he said, and passed out.

The Lark screamed with fury, levitated off the floor, and flew forward. She had almost reached Modeset's prone figure when a small fist like bunched metal slammed into her face.

Flicka stood over the duke, fists raised defensively. With the Lark still reeling from her blow, Flicka executed a low kick into the priestess's stomach and brought up her other knee to finish the job.

The Lark hit the ground, somersaulted backward, and leaped to her feet. Then she spun around with a backhand of her own, and Flicka, caught unawares, tripped on Modeset's arm. She fell to the floor, gasping as her hand crunched awkwardly beneath her.

"Foolish girl," spat the Lark, a second fire sphere already in her hands. She took aim, smiled grimly, and released it.

Flicka rolled aside at the last minute, struggling to her feet as the sphere exploded mere inches from the duke's unconscious form. Then, muttering an incantation under her breath, she raised both palms and sent two miniature bolts of lightning on a zigzag course toward the priestess.

Electricity filled the air and, for the briefest of seconds, it actually looked as if the Lark were in trouble. A wave of her hands quickly dispelled the illusion and she stood firm once again, shaken and bleeding, but still with all her wits about her.

"So . . . a fledgling sorceress," she said. "How . . . endearing. Your vampire offered no challenge; I wonder if you might?"

Without another word, she closed her eyes and levitated off the floor, arms held high and lips mouthing inaudible chants.

Flicka blinked and swallowed. She knew a little magic, enough to keep the witches away from the Fogrise water supply when she was a child, but she'd never read much beyond chapter four of *Migellan's Mastery*. This woman, on the other hand, looked as if she might actually know what she was doing.

A large ruby red mist had begun to swirl around the Lark, gathering pace as it developed into a swathe of cloud. The speed of the cloud intensified, swirling faster and faster until the Lark was nothing more than a shadow in the eye of the storm.

The room swam with magic.

The stone machine shattered.

Flicka prayed.

And Duke Modeset, having woken from his slumber, held aloft the silver saber (arm and all) and hurled it with all his might at the center of the cloud. Or else he would have done if his ancestor's appendage hadn't chosen that moment to take over.

The dead arm of Lord Bowlcock glowed a ghostly green as it floated on the air, saber raised high. Suddenly, it swung back and released the blade, which traveled at lightning speed across the room, spinning over and over on a fierce and unstoppable course.

There was a moment of silence in which the air

tingled so loudly that it set the duke's teeth on edge.

Then the magic died, instantaneously.

The Lark, blood leaking between her lips, staggered back with the sword protruding from her stomach.

"May the Great Yowler curse you all in your graves," she said, and died.

Flicka hurried over to the duke and flung her arms around him. Standing there, with his butler's daughter clinging to him like a limpet, Modeset made a startling realization that this was infinitely more terrifying than the priestess *or* the narrowly averted destruction of Dullitch.

This, he thought, is the closest I've ever got to a real woman. A voice deep within his subconscious added: something you're definitely going to have to rectify.

Flicka peered up at him through tearful eyes.

"I have something to tell you, Lord M," she said, sniveling.

"Go on."

"It's about Obegarde; I'm afraid he's dead."

FIFTY-FIVE

AN INTERESTING SCENE greeted Modeset and Flicka as they arrived on the landing below, dragging the unconscious form of Edwy after them.

They stopped in their tracks.

Jimmy Quickstint, looking dazed but aware, was standing over the trembling, obese guard that Modeset had encountered previously, the model blunderbuss pointed right at the disciple's groin.

"This is Moors," he said. "I think he wants to tell us a story."

"P-p-please don't kill me!" the disciple gibbered. "I don't know how I got involved in all of this! I only wanted to be part of something!"

Modeset glanced at Flicka and then stepped forward. "Do you know how we can repair the damage your lunatic cult has caused?"

Moors shook his head and blubbed. "N-n-no."

"Then we're not interested in mercy," continued the duke. "Jimmy, pull the trigger."

"No! Please! I'll tell you how to reverse the work of the glare machine."

"And return everyone to their flesh state?"

"Yes."

"How marvelous. And after that?"

Moors looked confused; sweat beaded on his brow. "I don't follow. . . ."

"Oh, you don't? Jimmy!"

The gravedigger raised the blunderbuss once more.

"Okay, okay . . . what else do you want?"

"I want to know everything," he said. "From beginning to end, start to finish, the whole pathetic story. You can begin with the reversal procedure."

It took a few minutes for Moors to stop sniveling. He plunged a hand into the pockets of the elephantine robe that draped his endless rolls of gut, and produced a small mirror on a chain.

"Mirror," he said weakly. "If the Batchtiki glares at you in daylight, it turns your flesh to stone. If its glare is reflected back to it, stone becomes flesh. Or so the scripture says."

"I find that hard to believe; my wrist guard reflected the lizard's stare directly. How come the lizard didn't turn to stone?"

"The Batchtiki are a species cursed by the gods. They can't see themselves. Well-known fact."

"Is it."

"Y-yes. We had to reverse a few glares during our testing phase. You just point the lizard away from you, hold a mirror up to it, and aim at whoever you want to be r-refreshed."

Modeset nodded and grabbed the chain.

"Very well," he said, turning to Flicka. "Take this and go downstairs to the room with the lizard cage. Change Pegrand back; be careful. When he's human again, or at least has returned to his usual state of equivalence, perform a similar ritual on the people of Plunge. Make sure they know what happened here, and who is responsible for saving them: namely us."

Flicka frowned. "You think they'll be grateful, Lord M?"

"No, but at least we won't get rocks thrown at us when we try to leave. Oh, and have Obegarde taken to the town chapel. We'll bury him here in Plunge; after all, he did try to save the place, and I'm sure the people here will show him more respect than any Dullitch citizen could afford."

Flicka started off down the spiral staircase, followed by Jimmy, who was still wielding the blunderbuss as if he truly believed that a vivid imagination could fire the thing.

"Right," said Modeset, turning with a snarl on the last remaining disciple. "Do you know what this is?"

He brought the arm round from behind his back and brandished the silver saber.

Moors shook his head; sweat was streaming down his cheeks.

"This," the duke went on, "spelled oblivion for your friend the Lark. Let us see what it spells for you."

He lowered the saber and allowed it to nudge the throat of Moors.

"Well?" he prompted. "I think it wants to know everything almost as much as I do. You're not going to disappoint us both, surely?"

"N-n-no. I'll talk . . ."

"Yes, you will. Go on, then!"

"I worked at Counterfeit House. I was lonely: no wife, no kids, and no friends. So I looked around for something to do, some kind of meeting I could go to."

"A meeting for sad, lonely people?"

"Yes . . . you must know what I mean. I can smell fellow unfortunates a mile off."

Modeset tried not to look uncomfortable, and applied the merest fraction of pressure upon the saber.

"Ahhh . . . all right! So anyway, I found this new group that had started up at the Yowler church. The regular worshippers got together on Friday nights, but I was always working then. The Holy Convocation of Lopsalm met of a Tuesday lunchtime."

"So you went along?"

Moors nodded. "The Lark was there, and Lopsalm. Mixer, the gnome, joined a few days after me; he was just a cleaner at the church, but they soon had him running round as an assassin. They chose him as the keeper of the great book, then faked a robbery so that the Yowler priests wouldn't get suspicious when it went missing. It was all the Lark's doing. She and Lopsalm were always conspiring, whispering to each other about some kind of deal they wouldn't let the rest of us in on."

"The rest of you? You and Mixer, you mean."

Moors wiped a globule of saliva from his fat lips.

"And Edwy," he blubbed, pointing at the prone figure. "He came last. He was workin' at the church as a caretaker, too. He'd overheard one of the meetings. They talked him into becoming number five."

"I see."

"And then, one night, they told us."

Modeset raised an eyebrow. "Told you? Told you what?"

"About the machines; that's what all the whisperin' had been about. They'd found this mad inventor who'd been thrown out of the Mechanics' Society. Somehow, among the three of them, they'd made exact replicas of the machines Doiley used in *Leaving Legends*, to turn the people of Plunge to stone."

"And you were shown these machines immediately?"

Moors nodded. "Lopsalm assigned us each a task. I was in charge of the reflecting machine, finding a place to hide it and then keeping it hidden. It wasn't too difficult; I used to be pretty influential in the guild. Edwy organized the church rota so that no one else found out about our Tuesday meetings. Mixer was supposed to tie up loose ends."

"Such as?"

"The thief brought the lizards, so he had to go. The Lark had friends at Counterfeit House who sorted out a high-level forgery for her; they had to go. The old inventor . . . well, you get the picture."

Modeset lowered the saber slightly. "The inventor was killed too?"

"Oh no," said Moors, heaving a sigh of relief as the edge of the blade drew away. "Mixer put the frighteners on the old fool, and we never saw him after that."

"Who came up with the idea in the first place?"

"Lopsalm, but really the Lark triggered it all off. During her time at the palace, Mistress Lauris had studied ancient lore. She discovered the Batchtiki, learned about their natural habitat. She even spent a few weeks in Grinswood checkin' up to see if the tomes were right. It was Lopsalm who suggested the theft; he's hated the dukes ever since he was fired from the palace."

"What? *Lopsalm* worked for Curfew?"

"No," said Moors. "For Vitkins. That's where he met the Lark. Then Lord Vitkins died and you came in, your lordship. They disliked you right enough, but nothing like they hate your cousin. Oh, they *despise* Mr. Curfew; say he isn't a patch on either you *or* your uncle; say he'll bring the city down."

"But the Yowlers put him in power!"

"They had to! He was your only relative. The main order won't get rid of him because he is of the blood. That's when the group came up with this idea of breakin' away from the others 'n' turnin' everyone to stone. S'posed to bring back Yowler, it was. Ha! They must've been mad, believin' all that rubbish. . . ."

"Yes," said Modeset thoughtfully. "Religion has a lot to answer for."

"It's not just that, Lord Modeset. *Nobody* likes Viscount Curfew. He's a spiteful man. Lopsalm thought the cult could make a difference, put him in his place."

"By turning the population to stone?"

"It seemed like a good idea at the time; Lopsalm and the Lark made it all seem so . . . noble. I never meant to hurt anyone."

"No, people like you seldom do. So, basically, Lopsalm and the Lark cooked this whole mess up between them, and you and your pathetic cohorts were merely pawns in their little game?"

Moors considered the question.

"Lopsalm's crazy," he said eventually. "I truly believe that. But the Lark, she knew what she was doing. I reckon she'd been planning to pull off something big for years. Fate probably brought the two of 'em together."

"Hmm."

Modeset stepped back.

"The people of Plunge will want an explanation," he said. "I'm sure that you'll be more than happy to provide them with one, after you've cleared up what little remains of your beloved mistress."

He licked his lips, turned, and headed off down the spiral staircase.

"And let this be a lesson to you," he called back. "Cults have a tendency to be manipulative and dangerous; so next time you want friends, try joining something sensible . . . like church."

FIFTY-SIX

REANIMATING THE PEOPLE of Plunge
turned out to be a tough (and largely thankless) task.
Most of them had little or no idea of what had happened, and therefore, upon regaining conscious-
ness, quickly came to the inevitable conclusion that
somebody had broken into their homes to point a
lizard away from them. It was hard to fathom, and
resentment was rife. Eventually, the mayor would
explain at great length just how much in Modeset's
debt they all were but, for the time being, chaos
reigned.

Jareth Obegarde was carried to a plinth on the
edge of the village, where a small service was per-
formed. The wound in his chest had closed, and his
eyelids twitched several times, but nobody seemed to
notice.

The service itself was nothing to write home about, especially since the Plunge priesthood had only a vague notion of what a loftwing was. Instead, they resorted to the more usual speeches full of useful phrases like "Rest in peace," "Take it easy," and "Don't get up for the milkman."

Modeset was the only mourner who cried, although Pegrand wasn't entirely sure that it wasn't due to the bite of the wind.

As the small group made their way back down to the village, they were informed that a raven had arrived, carrying an important message from Dullitch.

Modeset read it through carefully and smiled.

"Those wishing to be teleported back to the city by the all-powerful hand of the grand Wrickshaw Muldoon must stand in the town square at noon tomorrow. The city will pay a small recompense for anyone who quickly forgets the use of magic involved in this procedure."

"He must be quite the ticket, that wizard," Pegrand said, taking the note when Modeset proffered it to him.

"Are you serious, man? You've seen him—"

"Yes, milord, but he *did* get us all out here in one

piece . . . mostly. Besides, look, he's got letters after his name: G.O.F. What's that, Grand Order of—"

"It probably stands for Geriatric Old Fool. Now, do get a move on. We need to find somewhere to stay tonight."

FIFTY-SEVEN

THE FOLLOWING EVENING, Modeset released a giant raven from the highest window of Plunge Keep. On reflection, he could've sent the note back with Jimmy, but teleportation spells were dicey at the best of times and he couldn't risk *this* note going astray.

"Nice of Baron Herpes to let us stay here, milord," said Pegrand, straightening his jerkin in the chamber's angular mirror.

"It's Herps, Pegrand. Baron H-e-r-p-s. And we *did* save his subjects from being turned to stone."

"Well, actually, milord—"

"Yes, okay, we didn't. Satisfied? But at the very least, we turned them from stone back into flesh. Surely that deserves food, board, and lodging for a couple of days. Besides, this was once part of my land; that counts for something, doesn't it?"

"Of course, of course. So, what was the raven's message about?"

"A message to Viscount Curfew telling him about the Lark, her group, and the conclusion of this unholy mess."

Pegrand nodded.

"Where's Flicka?" he asked, looking around.

"She teleported back to Dullitch with Jimmy," Modeset said. "We're walking; it's safer, and besides, I've decided that we need the exercise. We should get to the border by noon."

It took a few minutes for Modeset's meaning to dawn on Pegrand. When it did, the result wasn't pleasant.

"We're going home, milord?" he exclaimed. "B-back to Fogrise?"

"Yes."

"Do you think you'll get the kingdom back?"

"Not without a fight, old friend, not without a fight. I was thinking that perhaps we might whip the peasants into a frenzy. Do you think they're the right sort for a revolt?"

"Dunno, milord. They're certainly revolting."

Modeset patted his manservant companionably on the back. "That's what I like about you, Pegrand. Your inimitable sense of humor. Did you manage to return the saber to the museum?" he asked.

"Yes, milord."

"And you apologized for the mess?"

"Yes, milord."

"And, of course, you helped clean up?"

"Absolutely, milord. I worked so fast, they couldn't see me for dust."

"Hmm . . . I'm sure. Then we're almost ready to leave. I'm going to thank Baron Herps for his hospitality. Do get a move on, won't you?"

Pegrand waited until the sound of the duke's footsteps had dissipated, and raised a defiant middle finger.

Duke Modeset, crossing the boundary between Fogrise and Plunge, looked out across a hundred acres of swampland.

"Home is where the heart is, Pegrand," he said. "A pity we have to go back to Fogrise, instead."

The manservant gave the question due consideration, and shrugged. He'd spent most of his life in the dreary little kingdom and harbored no particular desire to return there.

"Can't we just skirt round it, milord? I'm sure you'd get a hero's welcome in Dullitch."

Modeset looked incredulous. "The people of Dullitch are fickle," he exclaimed. "Besides, Curfew will invariably hush up any talk of our escapades. In fact, I doubt very much if the people of Dullitch will ever know just how close to oblivion they were; Curfew certainly won't risk any wrath from the Yowlers. All that aside, I can't sit by and watch someone else run my city. It's not my way. I'd rather return to my beloved ancestral home at Fogrise."

"You said you hated it, milord."

"Well, yes . . . but—"

"You said you'd gladly sit back and watch it fall into the swamp."

"Enough!"

Modeset's expression could've melted lead. Pegrand saw a fire in the duke's eyes that he hadn't glimpsed since the early days, when the kingdom still had a decent wall.

"We shall rebuild it," Modeset said, his voice determined. "Bigger, greater, and grander than ever it was!"

"Won't be too difficult, milord," said the manservant, on reflection. "Hut with a turret should do it."

"Did I already mention how much I hate you, Pegrand?"

"Frequently, milord. You old joker, you."

Modeset looked up toward the heavens, and wondered if the gods were laughing.

FIFTY-EIGHT

T HE THRONE ROOM at Dullitch Palace was enjoying the kind of silence that was merely a precursor to the inevitable din of someone losing their temper.

Viscount Curfew shuffled through a mountain of paperwork, gritted his teeth, and then threw the whole pile into the air. As pieces of tattered parchment drifted to the ground all around him, he snatched two at random and tried to read both at the same time.

"None of this makes sense," he groaned, glaring across the desk at Master Sorrow, who sat beside Jimmy Quickstint. "I have different accounts of the same situation, and a letter from Modeset flatly contradicting everything else. You do realize that I'm going to have to employ somebody specifically to unravel all this mess, don't you?"

"Sorry about that, sir," said Sorrow. "But it's a tricky situation. This is a very intricate case and these reports appear to have come at it from different angles."

"Yes, I can see that," agreed Curfew, scratching his fingernails over the rough wooden surface of his desk. "The investigator, Obegarde, wasn't it? He caught the gnome?"

Sorrow nodded. "Yes, Excellency."

"The gnome who carried out at least one murder on the orders of a man called Lopsalm, who you— Jimmy—witnessed commit suicide yesterday evening up at the cathedral."

The gravedigger, who'd managed to shrug off his usual gawp in the presence of royalty, attempted to nod but only managed a small cough.

"And according to one of these unfathomable statements," the viscount continued, "Lopsalm was in league with a young lady who, it now seems obvious, was referred to as Lauris or the *Lark*. Correct?"

"Yes, sir," confirmed Sorrow. "I read that somewhere in there, too."

"Good; it would appear my delightful cousin has dealt with her." He spent a few moments reorganizing the remaining papers on the desk before turning his attention back to the group.

"Let's see . . . Edwy, another member of this despicable order, and a man called Moors, are being brought up from Plunge for questioning? And we've also obtained a book from the gnome's hovel on Rump Lane. That, Mister Sorrow, would appear to be all she wrote."

"She, sir? There's a third witness?"

"An expression, Sorrow. Do not dwell on it."

"Yes, sir. No, sir. Won't, sir."

"Good."

"Can Mr. Quickstint go now, sir?"

Curfew nodded. "You can show him out, by all means. Just reward him and make sure he's doesn't leave town, so to speak. We may need his help to further document this matter."

"Yes, *suh!*" Sorrow stood to attention, saluted, and marched from the room without a second glance. After a few minutes he realized his mistake and returned to escort the witness away.

Curfew rolled his eyes and prayed for the day when he wouldn't have to deal with such glaring ignorance.

FIFTY-NINE

OUTSIDE THE PALACE, Jimmy Quick-stint stood watching the moon. The gravedigger felt itchy with excitement; he'd certainly had an extraordinary week. However, the sight of his old boss leaving the Dog and Duck did a lot to bring him crashing back to earth.

"Evenin', Mr., er, Coldwell," he ventured, praying desperately that he'd remembered the old man's name correctly.

"Evenin'."

"Nice night, sir."

"Aye," came the expected reply.

"Busy up at the cemetery, I'll bet?"

"Aye."

"Got another assistant yet, have you?"

"Nope."

"Lookin' for one?"

"Aye."

"I don't suppose there's any chance—"

The old man flicked his flat cap with a grimy forefinger. "Aye."

"I'll want better conditions, though."

" 's tha' right?" The old man swung his shovel over one shoulder and raised a bushy eyebrow. "An' what'd those be?"

"Um . . . an extra crown an hour."

"Aye."

"More help when I'm digging."

"How d'you mean, like?"

"Well, you could at least hold the lantern or something."

"Aye, ahright. That all?"

Jimmy considered all his demands.

"Yes," he said finally. "Well, also, I'd like to know who's sharing with my uncle."

SIXTY

I T WAS EARLY EVENING in Plunge, and rain poured in torrents over the sleepy town. In the makeshift graveyard that surrounded a solitary chapel on the cliff top, a gravestone toppled backward, slamming into the grass with a cushioned thud. A few inches from the upturned base, a fist erupted through the turf, straightened into a hand, and felt around a bit. Then it disappeared.

A voice from within said: "At least the sun's not out; that's something."

A few moments passed as the rain diminished into a fine mist.

Then the ground imploded, grass and mud spewing into the grave as Obegarde frantically clawed his way out. The loftwing, bare-chested but still clad in his trademark raincoat, rolled onto his back and took a deep gulping breath while the fine rain soaked into his flesh.

Nearby, a squirrel stopped assaulting a nut to watch him quizzically. Obegarde struggled up onto his elbows and grimaced when he saw the little creature observing him.

At the other end of the graveyard, an old lady tending a tiny grave beside the gates had frozen to the spot with fear. As Obegarde made his way past, he smiled at her.

"Nice day we're having, ma'am. Looks like I'm the first one up. Well, see you around."

The old woman's bottom lip quivered, and she forced herself to watch the stranger as he made his way down the road toward Plunge's town square. After a time, she turned back to her husband's grave.

"Henry," she said hopefully. "Do you know that man?"

THANKS TO:

My mother, Barbara Ann Stone, who watched me craft this book and prizes it above all others. My girlfriend, Chiara Louisa Tripodi, the rock of support to which I regularly anchor. Thanks also to Anne McNeil, who's lived in Illmoor almost as long as I have; and Joanna Solomon, who ably assists her. Finally, I must mention the legendary Irish comedian, Dave Allen, my first inspiration in the world of comedy writing. From the age of eight I listened to Dave describe life in his own inimitable style: nobody did it better. Dave, I'm glad you're still at large—this one's for you! (I'd also like to thank Susan Williams for obtaining Dave's permission to mention him here!)

ABOUT THE AUTHOR

DAVID LEE STONE was born in Margate Hospital on January 25, 1978, son of Barbara Ann Stone and Henry "Harry" Cooke. He was educated badly and therefore cannot by law name any of the schools at which this occurred (though one of them actually burned down before being relocated somewhere else).

After leaving school, David worked as a customer-service rep at a well-known retail outlet, and helped to bankrupt his mother's (then successful) real estate agency before searching for employment elsewhere.

These days, David can usually be found hammering away at a keyboard somewhere along the swollen lip of Kent, England. Beyond this, very little is known of the author, though he does have a small wart on the end of his left index finger.

The Yowler Foul-up is the second novel of the Illmoor Chronicles.

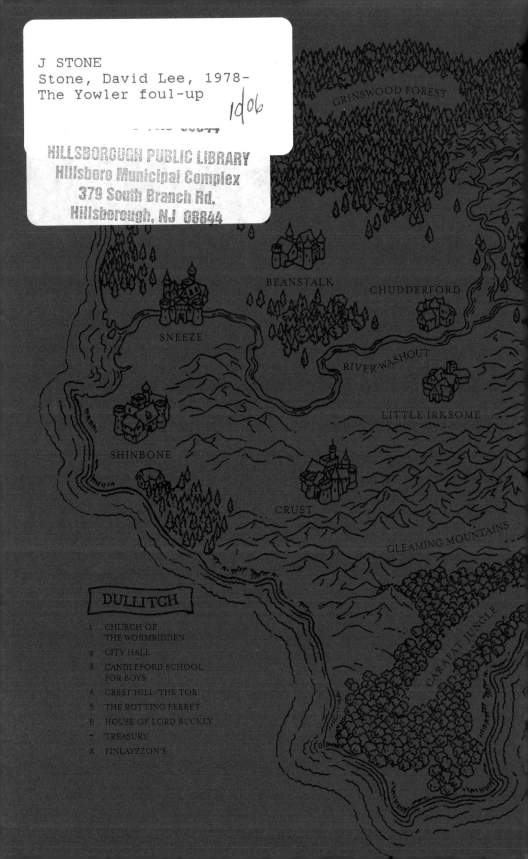

GRINSWOOD FOREST

BEANSTALK

CHUDDERFORD

SNEEZE

RIVER WASHOUT

LITTLE IRKSOME

SHINBONE

CRUST

GLEAMING MOUNTAINS

CARAFAT JUNGLE

DULLITCH

1   CHURCH OF
    THE WORMRIDDEN
2   CITY HALL
3   CANDLEFORD SCHOOL
    FOR BOYS
4   CREST HILL/THE TOR
5   THE ROTTING FERRET
6   HOUSE OF LORD BUCKLY
7   TREASURY
8   FINLAYZZON'S